A fresh assault wave closed in . . .

Hot blue muzzle flash lit up the darkness in stuttering, deadly pulses, exposing the attackers in their seamless black jumpsuits, their faces masked by the bulging plastic holographic night-vision goggles as they sprayed the corridor with flesh-shredding steel.

But battle-honed reflexes and powerful legs had already propelled Quinn out of the line of fire. Protected from the salvos of autofire by cement slabs stacked up against the walls, Quinn pulled commandeered fragmentation grenades from his combat suspenders and pitched them side-armed.

The strikers broke in different directions, but not quickly enough to avoid being caught in the lethal shrapnel burst zone. Hundreds of prefragmented, needle-sharp metal splinters penetrated their bodies from head to foot, ripping like demonic teeth through flesh and vital organs.

Also available in this series:

NOMAD

NOMAD

DEATH RACE

DAVID ALEXANDER

A GOLD EAGLE BOOK FROM

WORLDWIDE®

TORONTO • NEW YORK • LONDON
AMSTERDAM • PARIS • SYDNEY • HAMBURG
STOCKHOLM • ATHENS • TOKYO • MILAN
MADRID • WARSAW • BUDAPEST • AUCKLAND

First edition July 1992

ISBN 0-373-62116-7

DEATH RACE

The world turns and the world changes,
But one thing does not change.
However you disguise it, this thing does not change;
The perpetual struggle of Good and Evil.

—T. S. Eliot
The Waste Land

Author's Note

Accuracy in predicting the future is always a contradiction in terms. Nevertheless, I have aimed for it in the representation of the types of weapons likely to be commonly deployed in the early parts of the next century based on current trends, chief among which is a shift from the standard 9 mm round to ammunition in heavier calibers and/or with higher terminal ballistics properties.

Caseless ammunition and ultra-high magazine capacities are two other important trends in weapons design. Whether or not these developments will ultimately result in such innovations becoming commonplace by the year 2030 is, of course, a matter of conjecture at this point, but one which can't be ignored.

THE CAVE OF THE
MINOTAUR

Prologue

Griffin whirled around to confront the killer wearing the bull's-head mask. Corded arm muscles bulged as the creature raised the heavy broadsword and leveled a sweeping slash at Griffin's midsection with the keenly honed cutting edge of the blade.

The man-bull was fast and his blow had power behind it, but Griffin was even faster. Eluding the death strike, Griffin swung his own sword, hearing it clang against the cold black stone of the cavern wall as his opponent ducked under the glittering arc of steel to lunge at him on the follow-through.

Lined with lead against radiation and electromagnetic pulse effect, hardened against concussive blast with overlapping layers of armored steel and stressed concrete, the chamber was located deep beneath the wrinkled reddish-brown desert hills.

It had been built to withstand punishment verging on a near miss by a ten-megaton nuclear warhead and it had been carefully situated in a geologically stable area considered free from the threat of earthquakes or other natural disasters for at least a thousand years.

Officially the chamber did not exist. But many things that were officially nonexistent did in fact have a reality of their own.

The chamber beneath the roots of the hills was one of those things, and there was good reason for its classified status, for its official nonexistence.

For within the chamber there was contained a secret that could affect the lives of every man, woman and child on the planet. Perhaps the most dangerous secret in five thousand years of recorded history.

The masked figure laughed with scorn, the echoes of his laughter reverberating off the black stone walls as Griffin dodged down the tunnel.

The man-bull followed close behind, swinging the broadsword at Griffin's head.

Griffin dodged the lethal blow, which instead struck his back, the blade's keen cutting edge blunted on the armored understructure. Griffin followed through with a lightning counter-attack, drawing a short sword from his belt scabbard and plunging it into his opponent's midsection. Blood immediately began to gush in a dark, thick stream.

Bellowing in pain, the man-bull pulled out the dirk and began swinging his sword at Griffin, who parried the lunge and landed a blow of his own. There was a sharp clang as Griffin's blade sliced through the steel edge of the man-bull's sword.

The steady drone of life-support machinery filled the sterile white room. Soft violet light bathed its single occupant, the naked figure immobilized within the semitransparent cocoon.

Cables and umbilical tubes trailed from the unmoving figure inside the cocoon. A constant stream of nutrients and psychoactive drugs flowed through the umbilicals into the veins and arteries of the motionless body imprisoned within.

The cables were attached to sensor pads and subcutaneous implants, monitoring all vital signs from brain function to skin conductivity.

The Minotaur stared at the jagged stump, which was all that remained of his shattered sword. He hurled the useless weapon to the cavern floor and turned to run.

Griffin reared back, raised the blade above his head in a two-handed grip and plunged it into the man-bull's back, driving cleanly through muscle, lung and heart, its tip emerging crimsoned from the man-bull's chest.

Griffin pulled the sword from his opponent's body, and the man-bull crumpled to the cavern's stone floor. His masked head lolled from side to side before he stopped moving altogether.

Wiping the bloody sword on his vanquished foe, Griffin removed the bull's-head mask from the Minotaur's head. Below him Griffin saw the face that had been hidden beneath the mask all along.

It was his own.

THE TECHNICIAN inserted his key card into the reader slot. A microchip inside the key dumped its coded electronic data into the base computer as the tech was scanned in multiple modes. His identity established, a high-pitched whistle sounded, and he was permitted access onto the base.

The tech rode the elevator ten stories down to the lowest level of the ultrasecure facility. The control room was fully robotized. Humans played little role here, their presence no more than a conceit of the men who had designed the base.

The tech shrugged on his white lab coat, affixed his identity plate to the right breast pocket of the garment and went into the module. Printouts and other data pertaining to the functioning of the installation were waiting for him. He scanned the data, satisfied that all systems were performing within normal operational parameters.

Then he activated the node marked C.U.-129GR. The VDT showed him a series of graphs. He flipped through all waveforms, checking nutrient flow, drug levels and biological functions. All real-time processes checked out green. The clone continued to remain dormant. That status would soon change, however.

The tech reached into his pocket and brought out a paper-thin silver card. He inserted the card into a data slot located on one of the rack-mounted equipment modules beside him and keyed in a series of commands after it disappeared inside the scanner. The graphs and sine-wave curves on the VDT suddenly began to phase wildly as they changed shape and density.

With a mirthless smile the tech continued inputting command sequences.

*G*RIFFIN STARED DOWN *at the shattered hulk of his vanquished enemy lying immobile on the cold ba-*

saltic stone of the cavern floor, an enemy with his own face. Suddenly his field of view underwent a complete phase shift.

The cavern began to flicker and lose definition, like an image stretched on a lump of putty, while a sound like the buzzing of electronic bees began to fill his mind. Words and numbers scrolled on his IVD.

Copyright 2003. Cybertronic Robot Systems
Inc. All rights reserved...
Serial # C.U.-129GR
Sysgen...
Boot Sucessful...
Executing IVD Config...

The figure cocooned in the semitransparent sleep pod groaned. His spine arched convulsively and his limbs trembled and jerked as cables attached to them popped loose and fell away. At the same time the cocoon was lowered to the steel floor by pneumatic pressure.

The figure within continued to undergo convulsive fits as brain patterns spiked. Slowly these episodes subsided. The eyes came open.

Griffin sat up and looked around him. The IVD—internal visual display—was scanning the interior of the chamber, matching basic internal input/output system parameters against bio-organic and microprocessor memory.

Suddenly Griffin remembered where and who he was as a valid match configuration was logged. He slid out of the cocoon and walked naked down the long steel corridor and soon emerged into the sun-lit world beyond the electronic cave of the Mino-taur.

AT TWO-THIRTY in the morning, Jimmy-Joe and his two buddies, Earl and Bubba, were driving down the highway in Jimmy-Joe's Renegade four-by when the truck's headlights picked out a naked man walking ahead of them on the shoulder of the road. All three of them were returning from twelve straight hours of drinking and partying, and they were pie-eyed and feeling rowdy.

"Is he for real?" Jimmy-Joe asked his partners.

"Let's have a little fun with the guy," Bubba suggested.

Jimmy-Joe leaned on the horn as he swerved the vehicle to within an inch of the naked man. The guy stopped and stared at the truck as it shot past, and Earl, who was sitting up front with Jimmy-Joe, stuck his hand out the window and gave the guy the finger.

"Let's go back," Bubba offered. Jimmy-Joe made a U-turn and swung the four-by around toward the naked man.

"Hey, shithead," Earl shouted, sticking his head out the window, "public nudity's a crime in this state."

Griffin's glowing multimode IVD showed him a graphic overlay of the figure leaning from the truck. On its upper right quadrant a text box indicated extrapolated data regarding height, weight and body mass and the estimated age of the occupant.

"What are you, retarded?" Earl hollered again as he slid a Colt Mark IV automatic from the inside pocket of his shearling jacket. As Earl climbed out of the now-stopped Renegade, Jimmy-Joe and Bubba followed suit. "I'm talking to you, boy," Earl went on. "You answer my question or I'm gonna shoot your prick off."

Now Griffin scanned the other two occupants of the Renegade, the IVD showing that the closest somatotype match was with the driver. Earl cocked the black .45 caliber pistol and strode toward the naked man, then stuck the gun in his face.

"I think I'm gonna kill you, man," he said with a grin as Jimmy-Joe and Bubba snickered behind him. "I think you're gonna die, man," he went on, deepening his voice. "Unless you fucking *beg* me, man. Unless you get down on your knees right this second and lick the mud off my boots."

Griffin's right hand flicked out, grasping Earl's gun hand in a grip like corded steel. Pushing the gun into Earl's face a pulse beat later, Griffin pressed his finger down over Earl's, firing two rounds into Earl's face and blowing the front of his head into a mass of organic pulp and blowing that red, pulped mass out through the gaping exit wound at the back of Earl's shattered cranium.

Seeing what had happened to their friend, Jimmy-Joe and Bubba turned and made a break toward the Jeep, thankful that Jimmy-Joe hadn't turned off the engine. Shifting into four-wheel drive, Jimmy-Joe mashed down the gas pedal, expecting to hear the shriek of burning Bigfoot tire rubber as he peeled onto the highway.

It didn't happen like that, exactly.

While the Jeep's tires spun furiously, laying down rubber and spewing up clouds of acrid smoke, the truck stayed right where it was. The reason for this, Jimmy-Joe discovered as he glanced with terror into his side-view mirror, was that the naked crazy who had shot Earl with his own piece was now holding on to the rear fender.

Jimmy-Joe and Bubba jumped out of the four-by and ran aimlessly down the highway. Griffin let go of the fender, and the vehicle screeched forward, running Bubba down. As its front end collided with Bubba, instantly crushing his spine, the Renegade swerved off the highway and flipped over on its side amid the scrub-covered sand beyond the shoulder.

A fast sprint brought Griffin abreast of Jimmy-Joe, who'd tripped as he ran and now lay cringing on the tarmac.

Griffin needed Jimmy-Joe's clothes, or he would have shot him with the Colt. He didn't want Jimmy-Joe to bleed all over the clothes. Instead, Griffin closed his hands around Jimmy-Joe's neck and strangled him until his face turned blue-black and he stopped kicking and thrashing and lay still on the road.

Soon Griffin, wearing his new clothes, pulled open the left-hand door and stepped onto the side of the overturned vehicle.

Reaching inside the passenger compartment, he switched off the ignition. Then he righted the four-by and climbed behind the wheel, his IVD immediately displaying the map coordinates for the next phase of his mission.

MISSION LOG ONE:

Threat

1

"Yes, sir," the foxy female voice said. "We do show a credit to your account in the sum of fifty thousand dollars, U.S."

Dexter Barasheens was getting turned on by the lilt of the bank manager's Bahamian accent, and what she was telling him didn't hurt his ego much, either. He wondered if she looked as good as she sounded on the phone. Might be nice to find out one day, he thought to himself. He'd always planned to visit the Bahamas and party down the island way.

"You've been a great help," Barasheens told the woman. "I appreciate it."

"Glad to be of service, sir," she answered pleasantly. "Enjoy your day."

"You, too," Barasheens said, signing off and cradling the handset. He sat in the room in the Plateaus Hotel in Las Vegas, Nevada, without moving for a few seconds, letting the reality of it all sink in. He now had a hundred grand sitting in a numbered bank account, and all he'd had to do to get it was to push a couple of buttons and keystroke in a couple of commands.

Everything that Dexter had ever dreamed of doing was now on the verge of becoming a reality. He no longer had to work for anybody. He could travel wherever he wanted, whenever he wanted and however he wanted. He could afford to accept free-lance consulting work and not have to punch a clock. He could indulge in pure research, tack in any direction that appealed to him.

Of course, the heat that would be turned on by his actions would make the hundred-degree desert temperatures outside look cool by comparison. He would have to lie low for a while, preferably somewhere outside the U.S., some distant locale where his money could be stretched to the maximum.

No problem there. He spoke fluent Italian, French and German. He could pick his spots in Europe, the Middle East or Africa. Spain was a possibility. Even in the inflated economy of 2030 the Costa del Sol or the Balearics were still places where a man could live well and cheaply.

He'd already ensured that this would be so. The Bahamian bank account was set up under an alias, matching his new identity. The false passport and other ID had cost him a couple of grand, and so had the quick plastic job at an ambulatory laser parlor not far from his hotel, which had completely changed his features.

All were well worth the money.

Barasheens's plane to Sardinia was scheduled to depart McCarren International Airport in a couple of hours. Italy would be a jumping-off point for his later travels. With his identity completely changed, he now felt secure enough to enjoy the Vegas nightlife before he left. He might as well. Who knew how long it would be before he was back Stateside again, if ever at all?

First things first. Dexter checked the ammo clip on the 10 mm Glock semiauto he'd bought as a small health-insurance policy for his new life on the run. Then, raising the weapon and pointing it at the door of his room, he flipped on the built-in laser scope and watched the tiny red dot appear on the surface of the door.

Barasheens had limited experience with firearms, but it nevertheless felt reassuring to carry the piece nestled beneath his jacket, where he could reach for it in a hurry in case of trouble.

Flipping the laser targeter to auto-on mode, which would activate it as soon as he drew the gun, he made sure that the Glock's safety was switched back on the red dot before replacing the piece in the stiff new leather holster he'd bought to go with the weapon. Guns made him feel uncomfortable as it was, and there was no point in taking unnecessary chances.

There was a sudden knock on the door.

Dexter wasn't expecting any visitors and had not called room service. He had an odd feeling that he shouldn't answer the knock. The knock came again, though, and Barasheens decided not to allow himself to surrender to paranoia.

"Who's there?" he shouted.

"My name is Cathy, sir." Dexter heard a voice even sexier than the Bahamian bank manager's. "I have a bottle of champagne for you, courtesy of the management."

"You must have gotten the wrong room by mistake," Dexter called out.

"Oh, no sir," Cathy continued. "All first-time guests receive a complimentary bottle. It's our new policy."

Barasheens considered whether or not to tell her to go away or leave the bottle by the door. But his curiosity got the better of him. If she looked as good as she sounded, then he might prevail upon her to meet him later for a drink. Or better yet, join him right now.

He strongly suspected that many of the hotel employees would fulfill dual roles as occasional call girls, since the management seemed to have chosen them for looks, not experience.

"All right, just a minute," he said, crossing to the door to unlock and throw it open. As soon as he caught a glimpse of the person standing in the corridor, Dexter knew that he had committed a fatal blunder.

There was no female hotel employee named Cathy outside the door. Instead, Dexter stared into a hard, angular face dominated by a pair of coldly penetrating gray eyes.

Barasheens tried to shut the door, but the man outside moved with incredible quickness, shoving him inside and bolting the door behind him.

"Oh, my God!" Dexter cried, recognizing the intruder. "You're—"

"The name is Cathy," the hard man said in the same seductive female voice with which he had previously spoken. "I told you that before, sir."

The situation would have been comical had not Dexter realized that the man was a ruthless killer and that he himself was marked for termination.

Barasheens reached into his jacket and ripped the Glock pistol from its holster. As he withdrew the gun, its automatic laser scope painted a bloodred dot on the intruder's chest.

Barasheens pulled the trigger, but nothing happened. He cursed, realizing the safety was still in the locked position. He thumbed it back on and tried to fire again.

The intruder was no longer standing where he'd been. In a fraction of a second he had moved with fantastic speed to where Dexter stood pointing the Glock. Now the intruder's hand was on the pistol, a finger jammed behind the cocked hammer, preventing Dexter from firing the gun.

"Please," Dexter pleaded, trembling with a sudden, uncontrollable fear. "I'll give back the money. All of it!"

"The money is yours to keep," the intruder grated, now in a deep male voice as he wrenched the Glock from Barasheens's grasp and pocketed it. "In fact, you can keep it until the end of time," he concluded.

Picking up Dexter with one hand, the intruder carried him over to the bed. Dexter was powerless to stop the intruder as he laid him down on the bed and removed the Glock from his jacket pocket.

Dexter squirmed in the powerful grasp that pinned him to the bed, but his struggles were futile. The intruder fitted Dexter's right hand to the Glock's pistol grip and effortlessly shoved the muzzle of the gun into Dexter's own mouth.

The feel of the cold, hard steel of the Glock's muzzle jammed up against his epiglottis triggered an automatic gag reflex. Barasheens felt the powerful urge to vomit as his stomach heaved and his throat constricted.

"The angle has to be just right," the intruder said calmly, ignoring the frantic struggles of the man pinned beneath him as he slightly changed the gun's position in Dexter's mouth. "In fact, the angle is everything. Ballistics has to think you pulled the trigger of your own free will."

The intruder shifted Dexter's body on the bed and pushed his head to one side. "There. That's perfect," he remarked, and flexed his finger over Dexter's trigger finger, firing a 10 mm round up through the roof of Dexter's mouth and into his brain.

Barasheens's last earthly sense impression was the killer's cold, soulless eyes staring into his face with what he thought looked like the satisfaction of a craftsman having completed an especially difficult job. Then a supernova flared in his brain and everything went black.

Barasheens sagged into the pillow, which immediately began turning red as brain matter from the exit wound soaked through the pillowcase and foam filling. Sliding the bloody Glock from the destroyed head and dropping it to the floor, the intruder released his steely grip on the dead man and removed a suicide note from the breast pocket of the checked Western shirt he had taken from the driver of the Jeep a few hours earlier.

Before entering the room, he had written the note in Dexter's own spidery hand. Placing the note on the room's writing desk, the killer paused for a moment as if listening to sounds in the corridor beyond the door, then exited the room, hanging the Do Not Disturb sign on the doorknob, its wafer-thin digital display flashing large red characters.

Griffin turned and walked toward the elevator at the corridor's end, the initial phase of his mission now fully completed.

2

The climber was a slow-moving speck against the almost vertical face of the steep granite cliff. Sweat poured from his body, glistening on the corded sinews of his powerful arms as he stressed his already overtaxed muscles to the limits of endurance and well beyond.

From the distance he had traveled from the bottom of the cliff, Quinn estimated that there was at least another fifteen minutes of hard climbing between his present position and the summit.

He was running out of energy now but didn't slack off, couldn't afford to stop to rest. Instead, he picked up the pace of the climb, pushing himself mercilessly until his tortured limbs ached in protest and each beat of his heart came with the force of a hammer blow.

Twenty endless minutes later Quinn heaved himself up over the edge of the high bluff. For a while he lay on his stomach with his eyes closed, feeling his strength return, hearing the thudding of his overburdened pulse diminishing in his ear, feeling the fire in his calves and arms dwindle to a dull ache and the sweat beginning to cool on his overstressed body.

Only then did Quinn allow himself to stand up and look down as he untied the red bandanna that had encircled his head. He unrolled it and wiped the sweat from his face. The ordeal of the climb had been worth putting up with, for below him there now gleamed the mirrorlike surface of Lake Tahoe, reflecting the sunlight of a clear, bright autumn afternoon at an altitude of 6,200 feet above sea level.

Quinn knew then that every moment of the dangerous and difficult climb to the summit had been worth the punishment and the risk. The magnificent view had never failed to awe him or revitalize his mind and soul. Even after six years of devoutly returning to the region and making the arduous climb, the view never lost its magic.

The pristine wilderness of the western Sierras was one of the few places left in the continental U.S. where nature's beauty was still largely unspoiled by the pollution and overcrowding that had begun in the twentieth century and now, at the start of the twenty-first, showed no sign of abating despite decades of conservation programs.

Quinn slid the harness of the Verta-Flex pack from his shoulders and removed a pouch of trail mix and a plastic squeeze bottle of triple-distilled water. He sat quietly, legs crossed, drinking in mountains, sky and water as he munched his midday meal, the simple food tasting better than the high-priced buffalo steak he had dined on the night before at a trendy restaurant near the mountain lodge at which he stayed.

His hunger satisfied, Quinn next performed a chore that was routine in ordinary circumstances but unpleasant in his current situation. Nevertheless, it was a chore that needed to be done.

Quinn himself might be away from his office, but as sole proprietor of Intervention Systems—a security consulting firm with an international and semiofficial clientele—Quinn could never afford to be out of touch with business for very long.

From a pouch on his belt, he unshipped a small cell-net computer and punched in the code that allowed him remote access to his office mainframe some two thousand miles away.

Once on-line, Quinn scanned his bulletin board, noting incoming calls. Several had been logged in his absence, the voice messages transcribed into text by artificial-intelligence drivers that flashed these on the miniature screen of his palmtop.

Two of the callers required immediate responses. Quinn keyed in his messages and uplinked them to a comsat in low earth orbit.

An instant later his office computer had translated the text messages into simulated speech and was dialing Quinn's clients to deliver the voice mail along with an apology for Quinn's being unable to converse with them directly since he was enjoying a brief vacation.

Business having been dispensed with, Quinn again took in the scenery from his lofty vantage point.

To the east and west a curving ridge line traced the perimeter of the sparkling lake, earth tones and the intense blue of the sky meshing with the gray-blue of water into an interplay of muted light and shadow as the clouds shifted overhead.

Quinn would spend the rest of the afternoon exploring the ridge line, and toward evening he would descend to the lakeshore itself and make camp.

Next morning, at first light, he would hike back out of the wilderness by an alternate trail and eat breakfast at the lodge, forgoing the kayaking he had enjoyed the year before due to a regrettably tight appointment schedule.

Then it was back to the office and following up those computer-generated calls with personal messages and visits after an all-too-brief get-away.

THE LODGE'S LOBBY WAS quiet, and the deskman settled down to watch his favorite program of the day. He still kept an eye on the main entrance, but soon he was absorbed in the provocative flow of information, and his mind went on automatic pilot.

"This is Shawna Westmeyer for WNN—World News Network," intoned the attractive blond anchorperson. "Our cover story this morning concerns the question of the new technological wonder called ARGUS, or Armed Response Geosatellite Umbrella System. Some have called it a miracle, others madness. Perhaps what is most fascinating about ARGUS is that our government claims it doesn't even exist."

She paused and flashed one of her patented hundred-kilowatt smiles at the eight million households watching her that moment.

"But first a report on an issue of concern to us all. Telephone sex—can it be hazardous to your—"

Alerted by movement in his peripheral vision, the deskman looked up from the small HDTV—high definition television—screen. Two walk-ins had just arrived.

The two men entering the lobby didn't look like the usual tourists, though, the deskman thought.

Not the way they were dressed in dark business suits.

Not with the slack faces of those who had long ago lost the habit of smiling when making introductions.

Not with the hard eyes of those who spent their lives watching and listening to liars.

What they did look like was *trouble*.

"Can I help you?" he asked, switching off the TV.

The one on the right nodded. He was the older of the pair, with a jowled, fleshy face and eyes almost the exact texture and color of wet asphalt.

The young one could have been his kid brother, but the face hadn't yet gone as slack and the eyes were not quite as devoid of emotion.

The first man took an identicube from his pocket and placed it atop the front desk. He turned it on, and the eight-by-ten-inch hologram of a wanted felon appeared to one side of it.

"Recognize him?" the older one asked.

"Who wants to know?"

In response the man showed the deskman a card. The card bore the hologram of a bald eagle's head surmounting a shield containing a compass rose above the slogan And Ye Shall Know the Truth and the Truth Shall Make You Free.

Above the logo were three words: Central Intelligence Agency.

"You're no cop," the deskman replied. "I don't have to tell you a damn thing."

The younger man stepped up to the deskman and flipped open a black leatherette wallet. Inside it was a gold detective shield identifying its bearer as a member of the Las Vegas Police Department.

The deskman licked his lips and stared once more at the identicube's holographic image.

"Yeah, I know him," he said in a cowed, petulant voice. "The guy's a guest. Nice fella, too. Comes here every year."

Pretty soon the two men had secured the electronic pass key from the deskman and were going through the contents of the lodger's room.

While the older man examined the wardrobe, the younger man searched through what little luggage and clothing items they could locate.

"Do we wait for him?" asked the younger man.

"No. Those aren't my instructions," the other said with a shake of his head. "We take him out now."

With that he flipped the phone from his pocket and began issuing a string of rapid instructions into its mouthpiece.

3

Quinn set up camp on the shore of the lake. The granite peaks of the Sierras seemed to be on fire, glowing a vibrant, coppertone red as the orange disk of the sun hung low on the darkening horizon.

Having unrolled his sleeping bag, Quinn made a cooking fire out of a circle of stones and grilled the cutthroat trout he'd caught a few hours earlier.

He sat and ate the grilled trout, drinking black coffee from a porcelain mug and savoring the silence of the wilderness, silence broken only by the chirping of crickets and the occasional splash of a catfish breaking the placid surface of the lake every so often.

Quinn stood up to empty the grounds from the steel coffee percolator, facing away from the Chinese gong-size sun that glowed bloodred as it sank low in the western sky, when something glimmered for a moment off in the treeline on the high ground to his left.

A pulsebeat later, chips of pulverized stone sprayed into the air from a boulder at Quinn's side as a high-velocity round fired from a sound-suppressed sniper rifle smashed into it.

Had he not been alerted by the warning sun-flash, Quinn would have taken the round in the base of the throat. But Quinn was already sprinting from the strike zone. He had scooped up a small pack that contained vital gear, leaving his larger backpack, bedroll and cooking utensils behind as he dodged into the brush surrounding the edge of the high mountain lake.

The stuttering of automatic fire had joined the single reports from the sniper rifle as Quinn scrambled over loose rocks and the gnarled roots of lodgepole pine in a bid to put as much distance between himself and the shooters as possible.

In minutes the automatic-weapons fire had ceased, and Quinn knew he'd lost his pursuers. At least for the moment.

His lead wouldn't last long, he reckoned. Not if the hunters were professionals; not if there was logistical support for the pointmen; not if a dozen other variables he could not even know about were affecting the outcome of the hunt.

Sheltered by a granite ledge, Quinn paused for a few minutes in order to catch his breath and rearrange his gear, thankful that he'd taken the precaution of storing his vital effects in a small, separate carrying pouch.

America's national parks and wilderness preserves were no longer only recreational resources. Drug runners and psychos marauded through these areas in increasing numbers, and ambushes were not uncommon. Legitimate hikers did well to come prepared.

From his pack Quinn withdrew an H&K 10 mm semiauto. Though the pistol was compact, the 10 mm rounds it fired helped give it the range and stopping power of a much larger weapon.

Quinn climbed into a shoulder harness and eased the weapon into the leather holster. Magazine pouches containing spare ammo clips were slotted along the halters of the rig.

Armed now, Quinn sipped water from his flexible canteen and consulted his GPS. The satellite-uplinked, handheld global positioning system unit gave him an immediate fix on his location, indicating nearby highways and secondary roads.

There was no point in trying to return to the lodge. He could not safely assume that he was merely dealing with run-of-the-mill bushwhackers out to kill him and steal his valuables.

Not in his line of work, he couldn't.

In the course of his normal work as security troubleshooter, Quinn could count on running afoul of terrorists and other violent groups.

But now that he had again undertaken a mission as Nomad, tracking down and rooting out the megaconspiracy behind the Prometheus Net malfunction and blackmail attempt, Quinn was aware that the list of his enemies had lengthened by a considerable margin.

He did not bother trying to determine the nature of his attackers, either. All that mattered at this point was that they had tried to kill him. The wherefores and whys could be sorted out later. For now, first priority was evasion and escape.

Rising to his feet, Quinn began descending the high ground toward the junction of Highway 89 and I-80 indicated by the GPS liquid-crystal screen. There he figured he might flag down a ride to Reno Cannon airport and catch a plane back east. There would be time to file a police report and insurance claim later on.

Just then his phone beeped. Quinn thought for a moment and decided not to answer it, reaching into one of the seven pockets on his cargo pants to flip off the ringer select switch.

Whoever was trying to reach him could leave a message on his office voice mail system, to which they would be shunted automatically. If the callers were his pursuers, then he couldn't think of a better way to give them a fix on his position than by answering the phone.

Dusk had thickened to night by the time Quinn reached the highway junction. He huddled by the edge of the road, screened from view by the forest of lodgepole pine.

The road appeared deserted.

Quinn stepped out of hiding and scanned the blacktop ribbon for signs of approaching vehicles in both directions. Seeing nothing, he began walking in a northeasterly direction toward Reno.

Just then a helicopter popped up from behind a chain of low hills and, skimming above the desert floor, roared overhead.

Caught in the open, Quinn dropped to a crouch and raised the H&K in a two-handed, stiff-armed grip, but was blinded by the sudden glare of the powerful klieg light mounted at the chopper's undercarriage that flashed on and gave off an intense white light.

Quinn stood shielding his dazzled eyes as an amplified voice boomed down at him from above, out of the thundering darkness.

"Don't move," the voice instructed. "Lay down your weapon."

Suddenly Quinn heard the sounds of several vehicles come screeching to a halt behind him. Through the glare of the searchlight he saw more vehicles pull up in front, the circus lights mounted atop their passenger compartments flashing in a multicolored array.

Quinn now had no choice.

He was corralled.

He threw the H&K down onto the blacktop highway, where it made a hollow clattering sound.

A moment later he felt something strike him high on the shoulder. Glancing down, he saw the dart embedded deep in his upper left chest. Quinn reached up to pull it out, but the drug that filled the dart worked quickly and his hand grasped empty space.

Already reeling drunkenly, Quinn soon sagged to his knees, and the world folded up around him into a fathomless black ball.

4

He floated through a void filled with lights flashing on and off, the sounds of doors opening and closing, the smells of sweat and cigarette smoke, the unintelligible cadence of many distant voices all speaking at once.

He stopped, then started moving again, over and over again, until he realized that his captors had finally brought him to his final destination.

When Quinn began coming out of the drug haze, he heard the music. It was soft music, the kind popularly called ''celestial sphere'' music—swirling, flowing, synthesized mood music that some listeners claimed transported them to a higher state of consciousness and spiritual development.

Quinn felt himself being propped up by two heavyset enforcer types.

He could smell the musky odor of sweat rise from their overheated bodies as they dragged him through a stark white passageway filled with the swirling synthesized electronic music.

"This way," he heard one of them say. "That door on the right over there."

"Gotcha," the other replied.

Quinn felt himself pulled to the right and brought into the room. He heard the door slam behind him as he was deposited on his back.

Celestial-sphere music filled this room, too.

The cushions beneath him yielded to the contours of his body in strange ways, as though they were made of materials that could remember the shape of objects to whose shape they conformed.

Quinn heard the rasp of a noncarcinogenic cigarette being lighted by a tug on its ignition string and smelled the acrid smoke of synthetic tobacco. "Hey, Sam, how long before Maggard arrives?" the smoker asked after a long drag.

"Should be here any minute."

"Wish they'd invent noncarc smokes that don't taste like dried rat droppings," the smoker said with displeasure.

"You try Hyperions?" Sam asked. "They're supposed to be more like the real thing."

"These *are* Hyperions," the smoker replied, sounding twice as displeased.

Minutes passed and Quinn listened to the two hardmen making more small talk. Then the door swung open and the man they had expected, the one named Maggard, came in.

Maggard was accompanied by another man.

"How's our friend?" Maggard asked the Hyperion smoker.

He shrugged in reply, smoke curling through his nostrils, then stubbed out the butt end of the cigarette.

"Take a look," Maggard said to the man who had accompanied him into the room.

The doctor unshipped a bioscanner from his jacket pocket and aimed the snout of the pistol-shaped diagnostic unit at Quinn's face. As he squeezed the unit's trigger, Quinn saw a soft blue light glow at its tip through slitted eyes.

The doctor moved the scanning laser beam across Quinn's body, then shut off the unit.

"He's coming out of it," the doctor said as he consulted the screen of the remote microprocessor, which was linked to the gun by an infrared beam. The screen now indicated that pulse, blood pressure, cardiac activity and other vital signs were almost within normal limits.

"Yes, he's definitely coming out of it," the doctor said again as this time he bent forward and flicked a penlight into Quinn's pupils.

Maggard nodded at the two men who had brought Quinn into the room. They got up from their chairs and pulled him into a sitting position.

Quinn slumped sideways, and Maggard told the two to just let him lie on the slab.

"You should have answered the phone back there in the hills. It was me calling," he said to Quinn. "You could have saved yourself a lot of trouble."

Maggard pulled over a chair and went on in a gruff voice, "We're going to have to put you under again, I'm afraid. Before that, I just wanted to ask you why you did it, just for my own information."

Quinn made spluttering sounds and tried to sit up. Maggard motioned to the two hardmen, who raised Quinn to a sitting position on the low, cushioned table. This time Quinn was able to remain that way unassisted.

"Get me . . . a drink," Quinn rasped hoarsely, swaying from side to side and hawking to clear his throat. "Can't...talk. Drug...messed up my throat."

Minutes later Maggard handed him a paper cup drawn from a watercooler in the corner of the room. Quinn sipped from it, noting out of the corner of his eye that the doctor was loading a pneumatic injector with an ampule containing a colorless liquid.

"Again," Quinn croaked out, handing Maggard the empty cup. He shrugged, then brought Quinn another drink.

As Quinn slumped down, he rolled his eyeballs upward and could see that the two hardmen were paying him no attention. The smoker was fishing in the pocket of his windbreaker for his pack of Hyperions. The second man was playing a Gametron electronic arcade game.

Maggard extended his arm to hand the paper cup to Quinn, who reached out with a shaky right hand to grasp it.

But Quinn didn't take the offered cup.

Instead, his fingers clamped on Maggard's forearm with viselike strength as he simultaneously used the leverage of his legs to propel him up from the table.

Arm, leg and body torque combined to give Quinn the differential purchase necessary to swing Maggard into the Hyperion smoker, sending both crashing against the wall behind them.

The Gametron player swore as he dropped the beeping plastic square and reached for the SIG-

Sauer autopistol in a shoulder rig beneath his plastic jacket.

At the same time the doctor held the pneumatic hypo poised in his fist and ran at Quinn pole-vaulter fashion. A touch of the compressed-air driven hypo would be enough to put him completely out of commission.

But the doctor's action was ill-considered and worse for its timing. All the clumsy rush accomplished was to give Quinn the human shield he needed against the shooter, who was now sliding the compact autopistol from its holster.

Tucking right, Quinn grasped the charging doctor, spun him savagely around and sent him careening into the second gunslinger while Maggard and the smoker were disentangling themselves from where they lay sprawled on the floor.

In the process the pneumatic hypo touched the man armed with the SIG and released its charge of psychotropic agent through the epidermis of the thigh and directly into his bloodstream.

The gunman grunted as the fast-acting chemical took immediate effect. He let go of his weapon, reeled forward a few steps before his legs gave out entirely and then he toppled to the floor to lie in a helpless, writhing heap.

Quinn was out the door a heartbeat later.

To either side of him there extended an antiseptic white corridor whose "smart" walls displayed holographic murals of fantastic scenes of heaven while the celestial-sphere music floated through the air.

As Quinn dodged around the bend in the corridor, he saw the white-gowned men and women leading their hooded, blue-gowned charges into various rooms reached by doorways set along the corridor's walls.

Those wearing the hooded blue gowns had gaunt faces and vacant, hollowly staring eyes. Some of these figures were obviously psychotic, laughing hysterically and fidgeting convulsively as they were shepherded along toward different doorways.

Now there was no question in Quinn's mind regarding the place to which his captors had brought him.

It was an euthanasia center.

A house of legally sanctioned suicide.

The concept of self-termination had grown over the course of the past few decades to legalize suicide—even encourage it—as a solution to the problems of dealing with the terminally ill and the constantly growing legions of the homeless wandering the streets.

The momentum of public opinion had built until the lawmakers could no longer ignore it. A media blitz had advocated state-sponsored suicide as a humane way out for the homeless and the ultimate protection for society at large.

That also meant that Quinn could only be in Las Vegas, since Nevada was currently the only state in the Union to authorize euth centers and Vegas the only municipality in the country where two such centers were actually operational under the provisions of the National Eugenics Act of 2003.

But Quinn had no time for further consideration of his circumstances.

The men from the detention room were out in the hallway and desperate to recapture him.

He could hear their shouting voices draw nearer as they bolted through the corridor.

5

Looking left and right, Quinn began trying doors at random. After three tries he succeeded in finding one that was unlocked and slipped inside. The womblike circular room beyond was much larger than the one he had just escaped from.

Its curved "smart" walls were semitransparent, their millions of liquid-crystal display nodes painting an ever-changing array of scintillating patterns across their surface. From the hidden audio system there came electronic sounds that resembled the beating of a human heart.

"Peace be upon you," Quinn heard a voice suddenly say.

The woman in the white caretaker's robes appeared from a side chamber. She had Oriental features, and her black hair was cut fashionably short.

"Put this on," she said, handing him a blue smock the color of a summer sky.

"I'm looking for a way out of here," Quinn told her.

"Of course you are, my child. That is why you have come to the Las Vegas Temple of Forgiveness."

"Not that kind of way out," Quinn corrected the woman. "I mean a back exit, a service entrance, some place on that order."

"Why?" she asked, her tone suddenly changing slightly. "Who are you?"

Quinn looked at her intently, then shrugged, in no mood for answering questions after being shot at, drugged and kidnapped by homicidal strangers. "I need your help, and I don't have time to waste."

"Put this on," the caretaker told Quinn after a moment's scrutiny, again proffering the garment she had originally handed him. "It has a hood, which will help to hide your face," she explained.

Quinn shrugged into the loose-fitting robe and pulled the cowl over his head.

"Come with me," she told him when he had finished dressing.

Quinn followed, watching out of the corner of his eye as Maggard and the surviving hardman turned the L-bend of the corridor on a run.

"You seen a guy in street clothes go by here?" Maggard asked the woman. "Big guy, black hair?"

Quinn tensed and decided that he would first try to take down Maggard, who was standing nearest him, if the woman betrayed him. But as it turned out, he had no cause for concern.

"No, I saw no such person. Perhaps you might care to try our chapel." She pointed to the left wing of the corridor. "It's right in the direction you were going. It's interfaith, by the way."

Maggard grunted something obscene in reply.

"Come on," he then said to the hardman behind him, and they both took off down the corridor at a fast trot.

"Thanks," Quinn whispered when his pursuers were finally out of earshot.

A few minutes later the caretaker led Quinn through a narrow concrete passageway. Multiple electrical cable conduits snaked overhead, and thick bunches of copper-clad pipes stretched along the upper portion of the concrete walls.

When they came to the end of the passage, Quinn and his benefactor found themselves in a large concrete chamber filled with humming machinery. The woman led Quinn down a flight of steel utility steps to a fire door set in the opposite wall and told him to wait while she opened it and peered outside into the bright light of early afternoon.

"It's safe to go now," she informed Quinn after shutting the door again. "You hang a right at the alley, and you'll be out on the street."

"Why did you take the chance?" Quinn asked her.

"I don't know, but you interest me," she responded with a shrug. "Something about your face, I guess."

Quinn pulled off his gown and started to go.

"Wait a minute," she said in afterthought. "My ride's outside. Maybe you need a place to get away to, from those two men before, I mean."

Quinn didn't want to involve innocents in the deadly game of hide-and-seek he was playing with those who hunted him.

On the other hand, he was still groggy from the lingering effects of the drugging he'd been subjected to and still lacked a clear understanding of the reasons behind his being hunted and abducted in the first place. He needed somewhere he could go to ground.

"Won't you be missed?" he asked her.

She shook her head.

"I go off shift now, anyway," she told him as she removed the gown covering her street clothes. "It's okay, believe me."

The ride turned out to be a Harley-Davidson panhead. The dark-visored passenger's helmet masked Quinn's face as the woman pulled away from a parking spot and bumped off the curb and out onto the main avenue.

As they pulled into traffic, Quinn saw Las Vegas blue-and-whites stopped outside the main entrance to the Temple of Forgiveness and harness cops watching the procession of ragged losers shuffling toward its high glass doors with the hawk-eyed scrutiny of men who are on the lookout for one particular individual.

The woman drove the bike north along the casino strip on Las Vegas Boulevard South and into the residential end of the city, pulling into a parking lot of a multistory apartment complex off First Street.

She tucked the bike's ignition key into a compartment behind the license plate, explaining that she always forgot it otherwise.

At Quinn's prompting they took the fire stairs to her apartment on the top floor, avoiding the elevator entirely.

"Home, sweet home," she said to Quinn once they were inside the apartment. "There's some beer in the fridge if you want it. Help yourself."

Quinn opted for a soft drink instead and sat on the living-room sofa drinking the Siberian Lichen Cola while his hostess disappeared into a back room. Minutes later she returned, wearing a short black silk wrapper.

She sat beside Quinn on the couch and reached for a small blue plastic cube atop the coffee table.

"You do Jigglers?" she asked.

"No," Quinn replied.

"Mind if I indulge?"

"Go right ahead."

Reaching into the cube, she plucked one of the two wriggling bioengineered organisms from inside and closed the cube before the other could crawl out. Tilting back her head, she dropped the Jiggler into her right nostril and inhaled it.

"By the way, my name is Vashti," she told Quinn, shivering slightly as the Jiggler crawled into her brain and died, bathing the tissue with a powerful chemical stimulant. "You never did say what yours is...."

"Quinn," he told her.

"That your first or your last?" she asked, feeling the intense high hit her like a falling safe.

"It's both," Quinn said.

"You're a strange guy," Vashti told him with a laugh, peaking out.

"That's funny, coming from a lady who helps people commit suicide for a living," Quinn replied, sipping his soft drink.

"We turn away most of them," she replied. "We only accept the ones who have no other bona fide way out. In my opinion that's better than letting them go on as they are. Believe me, I know—I used to be one of them. The temple's way is faster and easier and probably more dignified in the long run," she finished.

"Yeah, you might have a point there," Quinn told her.

"But I did have an ulterior motive for bringing you here," Vashti went on. "Like I told you before, I find you interesting."

Saying that, she stood up and tugged on the slipknot of the thin sash around her waist, which held her kimono closed. Now the wrapper hung open, exposing her naked body.

Vashti shrugged, and the kimono slid off her slender frame and onto the floor.

"I think we both need a shower," she said.

"You like Tibetan?" Vashti asked Quinn a few hours later, turning toward him in bed.

"Isn't that what I just had?" he asked.

"Hell, but you're crude!" she exclaimed with a laugh. "Sexy, but *crude*."

She got up saying, "Seriously, I'm really hungry. There's a great Tibetan place that'll deliver. I have the menu ... let's see, it's in the kitchen."

Getting up, Vashti went naked from the bedroom. There was complete silence for a while, then faintly though distinctly from one of the rooms beyond, Quinn heard a dull thud.

Out of bed in a second flat, Quinn raced into the kitchen to find Vashti sagged against the kitchen sink. There was an unprettiness about her face, caused by blood streaming from the hole in her forehead. A man holding a sound-suppressed handgun had messed Vashti up.

The man wanted to do the same thing to Quinn. He aimed the weapon at Quinn's head and, with a broad smile on his sallow-jowled face, he pumped the trigger.

Two *pfitt*s, and the big plastic squeeze bottle of dishwashing liquid atop the sink counter at Quinn's right exploded, spraying the sink and refrigerator with white fluid. But Quinn was already across the room. He grabbed a cast-iron trivet from the wall and hurled it at the gunman.

His aim was accurate.

The gun went flying from the shooter's fist as the metal smashed against his wrist. Momentarily knocked off balance, he recovered quickly, a small backup piece snapping into his good hand with practiced ease.

Quinn lunged forward as the gunman brought his hands together to cock the slide of the backup gun.

The shooter had jacked a 9 mm hollowpoint into the chamber and was bringing up the gun in a crisp two-handed shooting stance as Quinn launched a toe kick that sent the weapon clattering onto the top of the kitchen table.

As the shooter went sprawling against a cupboard, he kicked up at Quinn and caught him in the stomach. Quinn tumbled backward, gasping for breath and seeing stars as he felt his back strike the metal edge of the sink counter.

The killer advanced on Quinn, wielding a knife he'd drawn from a boot scabbard. The lethal swing, fast and powerfully executed, forced Quinn to dodge sideways along the counter of the sink area.

The blade lashed out again, but this time Quinn caught his attacker's hand and rammed his forearm against the metal edge of the countertop, once, twice, then a third time, shattering the long bones of the ulnar radius and causing his opponent excruciating pain.

Nerveless fingers opened like obscene pink petals, and the edged weapon fell to the kitchen floor with a dull clatter.

A palm strike to the base of the throat sent Quinn's antagonist following his weapon to the linoleum like a felled oak, his windpipe crushed, splinters of jagged cartilage embedded in his neck.

Quinn realized he had only seconds before backup came on scene. He forced himself not to look at Vashti and instead searched the pockets of the gunman for weapons, ammunition and whatever useful thing he could grab.

These few seconds of slack time could make the difference between survival and destruction, because Quinn would have nothing for his own defense but what he could take from the downed man.

He found enough to suit him, including some cash, a cigarette lighter and a reload clip for the shooter's dropped gun, which he retrieved along with his discarded knife.

Grabbing his clothes, Quinn bolted through the open kitchen window, moments ahead of a two-man backup detail who had electronically picked the lock of the apartment door and were now bulling their way from the living room toward the kitchen area.

Quinn dodged flying parabellums and scrambled down the metal stairs of the fire escape as the strike team opened up with small arms. A spray of automatic fire shattered glass and pockmarked the woodwork of the window frame. He reached the parking lot moments later and found Vashti's Harley. He wasted no time retrieving the ignition key from beneath the bike's license plate.

The Harley's powerful big cube engine roared to life as Quinn kicked the starter, engaged the clutch, then swept out of the parking lot accompanied by the banshee shriek of smoking tire rubber.

Behind him a high-performance car with its engine idling tore off after the bike like a hungry predator spotting its fleeing prey.

6

Residential side streets soon gave way to the neon-lit tenderloin of Las Vegas Boulevard South, its billboards and signs strobing and flashing with a thousand come-ons.

The front end of the chase car that had taken off after Quinn stayed constantly in his rearview as he stitched in and out of traffic on the casino strip, then swerved the bike into the mouth of an alley in an attempt to lose the heat on his tail.

The wheelman of the chase vehicle was stubborn, though. Determined to follow Quinn, he cut in front of a van to his left, sideswiping its fender in the process, and bumped the sedan up over the curb to the accompaniment of blaring car horns.

Sparks flew from the chase car's undercarriage as it grated against the ironbound sidewalk and roared into the alley behind the fast-moving hog, the twin beams of its suddenly kindled headlights trained on the bike now only a single car-length ahead.

The chase car's wheelman floored the gas pedal, whipping the four hundred horses under the vehicle's hood to a frenzy as he narrowed the gap between his front fender and the Harley's rear.

The shooter sitting beside the driver had already whipped out a MAC 12 10 mm submachine gun and got ready to stick it out the window and vector out a put-away burst, but the driver put a restraining hand on his wrist and said, "Uh-uh."

The narrow alley didn't give the Harley anywhere to turn, and in another few heartbeats the chase car's front fender would collide with its tail.

Bullets wouldn't be necessary.

The smile on the wheelman's blocky face suddenly became a look of sheer horror. Through the service entrance of one of the restaurants fronting the alley, he saw an iron-sided Dumpster full of trash suddenly trundled directly in front of the car a fraction of a second after Quinn had sped past that same doorway.

Frantically he hit the brakes, but there was no lead time left to stop the big, heavy car.

With the shriek of tortured rubber echoing off the alley walls, the chase car crashed headlong into the side of the Dumpster, its momentum skewing it around so that its rear section smashed into the wall of a building on the opposite side of the alley.

The car's fuel tank ruptured, and a spark caught the gasoline spurting from the rift. The driver and the gunman beside him struggled to pull themselves out from under the airbags that had ballooned up from the steering column and doors, but a second later their car exploded into a big ball of fire.

Passersby could do nothing but stand and gape as a cocoon of crackling flame engulfed the crashed vehicle. They could only stare in horror at the dark, thrashing figures of the two men trapped inside the burning passenger compartment and listen to their screams of agony.

Idling at the alley's opposite mouth, Quinn established that the chase car had been totaled. With the kill crew now off his back, he goosed the hog and roared up the avenue toward the city limits.

"THAT'S HIM! Step on it!"

A police cruiser picked up the wanted vehicle about a quarter mile away from the interstate. This was the same cycle reported tearing down the casino strip and involved in the big crash only minutes prior to the sighting.

"No screwups this time," the law officer in the shotgun seat said to the driver.

"Don't worry," he replied, flexing his fingers into the driving gloves he'd just slipped on, "there won't be."

Five minutes of redlining the Harley, and Quinn was flying down I-15, arrowing into the wrinkled hills rising beyond the broad flatlands on which the city had been built by organized crime decades before, a place called the Valley of Fire because of its flamboyant red sandstone formations.

Darkness was falling now and falling quickly. Quinn was well beyond the city limits, racing the bike through rough desert country, when suddenly he heard the police siren behind him and saw the flashing lights in his rearview.

The cops were fast.

They were gaining on him quickly.

Quinn's digital speedometer showed him doing one hundred twenty-five miles per hour, which meant the cops were doing as much or better.

"Don't lose him," the harness bull beside the driver of the police car down the road said, his combat shotgun slung across his lap, "we got him cold."

"No problem," the driver replied. "Unless he goes off the road."

At that moment Quìnn himself was considering doing just that. When he spotted the unpaved secondary road that was coming up fast on his left, his mind was made up. Swerving the hog onto the side route, he would try dirt-tracking the squad car.

With clouds of yellow-brown desert dust billowing in their faces and the police vehicle's suspension system bumping over the rutted old road, the cops were soon forced to slow down and were quickly outdistanced by the speeding bike.

Suddenly Quinn heard an ominous sound, which rose to a crescendo pitch above the steady roar of the Harley's powerful engine. Quinn looked up and to his right and saw the mechanized black dragonfly rising menacingly above the wrinkled red hills.

The helicopter was a Commanche attack chopper. Small, black and very deadly. It vectored in on Quinn, and suddenly a salvo of automatic fire from its nose turret gun screamed down onto the road surface. Quinn poured on the RPMs, the Harley bolting away from the strike zone like a whipped stallion.

Behind the bike, the squad car wasn't as lucky.

Glowing red tracers ripped down through the twilight and punched through the windshield of the police car, killing the driver instantly.

The man on the right grabbed for the wheel, but it was too late to stop the speeding vehicle from doing a three-sixty barrel roll and then go bouncing and spinning into a dry arroyo.

The cruiser crashed into jagged boulders on the flat bottom and came apart with a tearing of metal.

More agile than the four-wheeled vehicle, Quinn's Harley bounced across the uneven surface of the rocky desert floor as the killer chopper pursued it with a vengeance.

Then the air filled with a series of thunderclaps as multiple rocket strikes sent chunks of shattered rock and tons of displaced sand spewing skyward in a thick brown cloud. Quinn tore a zigzagging course through the pattern of ground-shaking detonations, regaining the road and shooting forward.

The helicopter followed in determined pursuit, effortlessly keeping him in sight from its aerial vantage point.

As Quinn crested a shallow rise, he could see what appeared to be a fenced-off complex of low-rise concrete block buildings at the end of the private road.

Signs posted on the gates identified the area as a government installation and warned against trespassing.

Quinn ignored these threats, having far more pressing ones to contend with.

Putting on a burst of speed, he aimed the bike toward the gate but was thrown clear as another explosion erupted to one side. The bike went roaring off into the gloaming and crashed into the chain-link fence.

That accident probably saved his life.

The helicopter let fly a Hydra rocket round, whose IR-seeking head tracked on the hot tailpipe of the stray Harley, blowing it up and gouging out an enormous crater.

Quinn was unscathed as he scrambled over the fence and toward a concrete blockhouse rising out of the desert landscape as the flaming red sun passed silently behind the hills surrounding the Valley of Fire.

The rust-flecked iron door set in its face was securely bolted and locked.

Using the commandeered handgun, Quinn shot off the lock and tore at the door. It opened with a shrill, protesting shriek of tortured metal.

He just made the dark stairwell beyond the door as the helicopter banked sharply and launched another Hydra salvo from a stationary hover.

Quinn heard another loud explosion and was almost sent falling down the steel steps by the concussion of the blast front, which hit with such a terrific wallop that it made the ground around him shudder and quake.

Knocked from his hand as he went crashing against the wall of the stairwell, the gun went clattering down the stairs and was lost from sight.

Regaining his footing, Quinn charged down the steps, and soon the darkness engulfed him.

"NO SIGN OF TARGET," the pilot said into his commo unit. "He's inside the complex, over."

The strike manager, sitting in a Vegas hotel room and talking into a palmtop signal-hopping commo unit, considered his present options.

There wasn't any more than a *single* option, really. He had to send in the commando strike unit to accomplish what air power alone apparently could not.

It was that or let Quinn escape.

"Okay, take the bird out of there."

"Wilco," the pilot replied, and banked the Commanche, withdrawing from the area.

Minutes later a second helicopter, this one a Blackhawk slick carrying two four-man teams, set down near the site, which was part of the sprawling system of MX tunnels originally started in the early eighties but never completed. The massive underground system of rails were planned to shunt missiles around so that the Soviets would never be able to pinpoint their location. But with the lessening of the Cold War, the original plan was eventually abandoned.

Each strike team was equipped with night-vision goggles and Spectre 9 mm SMGs, each with high-capacity 50-round clips.

The first team deployed down into the tunnel via an entrance giving access from the side of a mountain farther to the northeast of the entrance Quinn had used. The second team was dropped to the south of where Quinn had entered.

The teams began fanning out through the twisting corridors.

Eventually they would catch Quinn in between them. Then they would slam the hammer against the anvil and crush Quinn flat.

Their orders were to terminate on sight. All were pro enough not to question those orders.

7

Quinn now had little choice but to penetrate deeper into the dark maze of deserted tunnels and concrete bunkers, which ran on for miles beneath the deserts of Nevada and Utah.

No line of retreat was left to him. The pathway by which he had entered the complex had been blown to rubble by the final missile burst.

On the sands above, unknown assailants who sought his death for reasons only they knew would be busy forging new plans to snuff out his life.

But in the process of boxing Quinn into a corner, the opposition had narrowed their own tactical options, too. The helicopter pilot had miscalculated by firing a Hydra round directly into the tunnel's surface accessway.

By taking this action, he had effectively sealed it off to penetration by a search-and-destroy team. The blast had entombed Quinn inside the dark labyrinth, but it had effectively bought him valuable lead time.

Nomad's pursuers would now need to locate and deploy via alternate routes into the subterranean network of concrete-walled passageways.

As for Nomad, his sole hope of evasion and escape lay in finding a way out of the tunnel complex not covered by his pursuers—if one existed at all, of course.

Quinn was encouraged by the faint eddies of air that he felt wafting over his face.

If there were air passages leading to the surface of the desert above him, then he reasoned that there might also be side chambers large enough for a man to negotiate and make his escape.

Quinn had lost his gear pouch when he had first been taken. He carried no weapon now that his gun had fallen into the bottomless darkness during the rocket strike.

But he found something in his pocket that could mean the difference between survival and death. This was the cigarette lighter he had retrieved from the pocket of the downed gunman just before fleeing from Vashti's apartment one step ahead of the killer's backup.

Quinn thumbed the flint wheel and looked around in the dim light given off by the lighter's small, guttering flame.

The chamber was immense, he saw at once, and it trailed off into Stygian darkness. Where slabs of concrete had fallen away, Quinn could discern the rusted brown gridwork of the walls' steel reinforcements.

Electrical cables and power conduits dangled impotently from the ceilings. Stagnant groundwater lay in cold, gray pools on the concrete deck.

There were also side corridors branching off the bunker in which he stood, leading away in all directions, undoubtedly linking up with other main branches of the sprawling tunnel complex.

More light was now a necessity. A single misstep, and Quinn could fall right into a pit and break his neck or injure himself too severely to move and thereby starve to death.

Closing the lighter's lid and extinguishing its flame, Quinn stripped off his shirt. He picked up an iron rod—scrap left over by workmen who had excavated the tunnel—and tightly wound the garment around one end of it to produce a makeshift torch. He tied the shirt tightly with strips cut from his pants leg with the knife taken from Vashti's killer.

He wet the fabric with fluid from the lighter, ignited it and held the torch aloft. The foul-smelling flame gave off an uneven light, but it was better than nothing.

Quinn noted that the torch's flame seemed to be faintly drawn in the direction of a side tunnel to his immediate left. For want of a better direction to take, he started to proceed along it.

ELSEWHERE IN THE VAST tunnel complex, strike units Eagle and Foxbat were moving into position.

The four-man teams were being deployed to the north and south of the entrance via which Quinn had penetrated the tunnel network.

Moving with caution, the first strike unit progressed slowly down the length of the tunnel.

The holographic infrared-sensitive NVGs worn by each member of the search-and-destroy crew provided all personnel with perfect vision in the nearly lightless conditions that prevailed in the network of subterranean passageways.

The covert strikers carried P-90 close-assault weapons. Compact, firing high-velocity 5.70 x 28 mm rounds and with virtually no recoil or muzzle climb, the CAWs were perfectly suited to the operational particulars of deployment in such restricted surroundings.

As the two strike teams fanned out through the branching network of side corridors, Quinn was meanwhile negotiating the tunnel complex by the light of his guttering torch.

The passageway that he followed soon came to an abrupt end, opening out into empty space. Peering out over the ledge of the opening, Quinn saw a huge chamber yawn beyond it with circular walls and a high, vaulted ceiling.

He supposed that this might have been originally planned as a service bay for heavy equipment or personnel quarters.

Driven into the corrosion-stained concrete wall of the chamber was a row of rusting iron cleats that began about a foot below the opening and extended to the chamber's bottom.

Climbing down this ladder, Quinn descended to the deck of the concrete bunker.

From his new vantage point he could discern the shadow-shrouded mouth of a smaller, narrower tunnel leading away from it, which he had not been able to make out at all in the pitch darkness from his previous position many yards above the floor of the pit.

Quinn followed this new tunnel.

After a few hundred yards it cut left, then skewed to the right before straightening while angling slightly upward on a shallow grade.

Quinn also began to take note of the fact that the currents of air he had felt earlier in his odyssey through the labyrinth were becoming stronger, as though he was nearing a large air passageway leading to the surface.

But after almost an hour of negotiating the tunnel, Quinn found himself still no closer to finding a way out of the maze. It was a depressing, though not especially surprising, turn of events, since the tunnel complex meandered on for dozens of miles.

Apart from this discovery, his guttering torch now showed signs of failing entirely as the fuel-soaked fabric was consumed by flame. Before the torch went out entirely, Quinn made sure to establish his final bearings.

He took in the fact that he stood within a square, high-ceilinged concrete bunker that had tunnels branching off at its left and right. By the torch's diminishing light, Quinn followed one of the tunnels, which brought him into a larger vault with circular walls that appeared as though it might have been intended to house an operations center of some sort.

Gutted emplacements for banks of rack-mounted computer terminals, rusted from exposure to mineral-laden groundwater that periodically flooded the tunnels, stood forlornly at odd points in the huge chamber, although most of the equipment had been stripped from the steel framework. He committed his position to memory as his torch flared once then abruptly went out.

Suddenly Quinn heard the sounds.

The sounds of the hunters.

They were still faint, to be sure, half-heard echoes originating from deep in the eternal night of the branching tunnels, but he recognized them as coming from no other source than those who pursued him.

The slow, steady cadence of boot leather on concrete had made those sounds, and Quinn knew that the men who stalked him through the shadows were moving in from the leftward tunnel he had not taken.

He realized that had his torch not gone out, he would have been at the mercy of commandos, who were almost certainly NVG-equipped. He would have been the perfect stationary target for a lethally placed round.

Quinn stood stock-still, barely breathing. There were deep grooves gouged into the walls by cutting machines, niches intended to house banks of intelligent battle-management equipment, and he crept into one of these.

Pressed into the niche like a soft-shelled animal taking refuge from a predator in a rock crevice, Quinn waited and listened. Minutes later the pointman of team Foxbat entered the bunker. Behind him filed the other commandos, all moving slowly as they crossed the chamber, night-seeing specters who stalked their prey through the timeless darkness.

Quinn's vision had adjusted to the shadows by now. Even in pitch darkness some photons of light stayed in the environment, photons that the eye could detect.

As the hunters drew nearer, Quinn could make out the black silhouettes of their bodies, vaguely discerned through the mote-flecked darkness of the tunnel.

As the last of the figures passed his position, Quinn made his move. Hurling a piece of loose rubble across the concrete deck, he watched as the figure to his right spun around in response.

The NVG-equipped death-stalker pointed the P-90 in his hand in the direction of the sudden sound. His electronic battle mask canted sideways, invisible lasers probing the darkness in pursuit of target acquisition.

The hunter's holographic NVGs showed him nothing, though. He reached up and studded the night-seeing mask to a new setting, one that peered into the infrared and detected the thermal signature of living beings against the cool background of insensate stone.

Glowing red, green and blue, the figure of a man sprang suddenly into the striker's field of vision. The hunter swung his weapon toward it, squeezed its trigger, tried to kill the glowing phantom in the darkness. But it was already too late for him.

Quinn was already behind the striker, one hand holding him in the viselike grip of a choke hold as he ripped the night-observation mask from his face.

The striker grunted, seeing random shapes and colors flash in the enveloping darkness due to the shock of the sudden shift from electronically augmented viewing to using his own naked eyes.

Now the killer was blind. He was a thrashing Cyclops whose strength had resided in the power of his extinguished electronic eye.

Without it he was now virtually helpless.

Quinn pivoted to face his opponent, who was bringing the P-90 into play, whipping it from side to side as he struggled to discern the enemy in the darkness. Quinn struck savagely—struck to kill. A spinning side kick smashed into his enemy's hand, sending the weapon flying.

Following through on the sudden foot blow, Quinn launched a knife-fingered hwa-rang-do thrust to the opponent's larynx, following this attack with a series of knuckle blows to the face.

The striker was knocked backward against the wall, blood spurting from his nostrils as he howled in pain in the primeval terror that men know at the nearness of death.

Having delivered the flurry of hand blows, Quinn smashed his fist up into the striker's rib cage and into his unprotected heart region.

He felt the heart of the hunter beating there and he squeezed the living organ with his hand. The heart ruptured, bursting apart within its hemispherical cage of bone. His chest cavity filling with hot aortal blood, the striker sagged to the deck, dying like an animal in the dark.

"Any problem, Jarvick?" a voice said from the ground.

Breathing hard, Quinn took the crackling commo unit from the dead commando and gripped it in his hand. The request was repeated by the strike team leader.

"False alarm," Quinn said in a gruff voice that he hoped would pass for the taken-down Jarvick's. "I'll catch up."

"Roger," said the unit leader, evidently accepting Quinn's impersonation.

Now Quinn worked rapidly and determinedly, fitting the striker's holographic NVGs to his own head and commandeering his P-90 CAW and the load-bearing suspenders containing ammo, grenades and other vital survival equipment.

The most important discovery of all was the GPS unit carried by the downed commando in a Velcro case. The GPS was not only uplinked to an orbiting navsat, but it had the map of the tunnel system programmed into its on-board microprocessor input/output system.

Quinn was able to figure out how to access the navigational data in seconds. He saw at once that he had been on the wrong track and that the side tunnel nearby was actually his way out. The tunnel branch that he had been about to take when he had been sidetracked by the approach of the hunters would have only looped him back in the direction from which he had originally come.

Moving with a speed born of desperation, Quinn sprinted down the tunnel's length. This time his NVGs showed him the way with perfect clarity. But he had to move fast, had to push himself to maximize his chances.

It was only a matter of time before the rest of the strike team realized that the commando named Jarvick was down and that Quinn, wearing his uniform, was now stalking them.

8

Clothed in black, P-90 armed and NVG-equipped, Nomad slipped through the night world like an avenging specter toward the farthest tunnel entrance marked on the GPS liquid-crystal readout panel.

He had ventured only a few hundred yards from his last position when he overheard an exchange over the commo unit he'd taken from the terminated man-stalker.

"Jarvick, where the hell are you?" the team leader was asking. The other members of the strike detail had already reached their linkup point. Only Jarvick was missing. Something was not right.

This time Nomad did not respond to the strike team leader's request for a position update. Failure to acknowledge the order would cause the search-and-destroy teams to realize that one of their number had been taken out, but to acknowledge his position at all would only accomplish the same end.

Let the bastards guess, Quinn thought.

Let them wonder.

"Deploy to grid sector 1010-delta using tunnel branch eighteen north," the strike leader said over the comlink, an edge of nervousness in his voice. He punched up the last-known coordinates of the missing striker on his GPS and cross-checked this position against the schematic diagram of the tunnel complex stored in silicon memory.

"Our target is somewhere in that sector," he went on. "Use extreme caution. If he took out Jarvick, then he's now armed and I don't have to remind you that he is highly dangerous."

Quinn switched off the comset. He had heard enough. He had to act and think quickly now.

The remainder of the strike team, and possibly backup, too, would be closing in on him. They knew that he was located—*trapped* was an even more accurate term—in a sector of the tunnel complex within confined limits accessible by only a handful of branch conduits.

Making better time now that he could see clearly in the darkness, Quinn nevertheless only managed to cover a short distance when he saw two strikers materialize from a feeder tunnel a few dozen feet ahead of him in the darkness.

Emerging from the shadows, the pair of strikers spotted him instantly, Quinn's glowing electronic image visible on their NVGs against a gray raster field.

The first striker acquired Quinn, white cross reticles skewing across the photonic gray background and flashing as the target was framed in the killbox.

At that point he opened up with the P-90 in his gloved hand. His reflexes had been sharpened by long hours spent in assault-training simulators launching high-terminal ballistic bullets through space, but in the given situation he failed to hit his fast-moving target.

Quinn broke for the protection of a pile of rusted I-beams left by the construction crews when work on the tunnels had been abandoned decades before.

Hunkering behind the cover of the beams, he was temporarily screened from fire as ricochets spanged off into the darkness, throwing off hot white sparks.

He snapped back P-90 suppressing fire of his own in answer to the offensive burst, watching the shapes pivot and dodge from the glowing white box at the center of his raster field.

The net result of this tactic was to force the shooters to break for cover themselves and flatten against the unfinished concrete walls after retreating into the mouth of the feeder tunnel.

Quinn used the seconds that this maneuver had bought him to move speedily away from the hot zone, following a ramp that sloped down to his right. He had no chance of reaching his destination, he was now fully aware.

The GPS had shown him that another exit was located farther south. He would have to make for the second exit if he was to stand any chance of escaping the assault.

But the two battle-masked terminators had other plans for Quinn, plans that called for abruptly bringing his life to a bloody end in the savage night world.

The two whom he had come up against had relayed their position back to the strike manager, and the second hit detail was already closing in fast, navigating by way of their global positioners.

Quinn walked right into another two-man death detail before he could take evasive action as the blacksuited commandos loomed up ahead of him from the dark maw of a tunnel.

Life went to Quinn. Though he was as surprised as the opposition, he managed to shoot first, throwing up a zigzagging wave front of high-energy rounds. Death went to the two strikers, whose fire went wild as they were struck repeatedly by Nomad's terminating patterns of whipsawing steel.

Grabbing up extra reloads from the downed shooters, Quinn continued quickly along the tunnel in the direction that he had been originally proceeding.

He encountered no further opposition for several minutes, and then the darkness brought a fresh assault wave of death-bringers.

Three more strikers were emerging from a gaping rupture where a section of tunnel had fallen away due to geological instability, exposing a huge, ragged fissure in the concrete walls through which groundwater constantly drained.

Hot blue muzzle-flash lit up the darkness in stuttering, deadly pulses, exposing the hunters in their seamless black jumpsuits, their faces masked by the bulging plastic bubbles of glowing holographic NVGs as they sprayed the corridor with flesh-shredding steel.

But by the time they fired, battle-honed reflexes and powerful legs had already propelled

Quinn out of the lance line of metal studs. Protected from the salvoing autofire by concrete slabs that had been stacked up against the walls, Quinn pulled commandeered fragmentation grenades from his combat suspenders and pitched them forward with a sidearm delivery.

The strikers broke in different directions but not quickly enough—not nearly quickly enough to avoid being caught in the lethal shrapnel burst of the detonating submunitions.

Hundreds of prefragmented, needle-sharp metal splinters penetrated their bodies from head to foot, ripping like demonic teeth through flesh and vital organs to induce almost instantaneous death.

Before long Quinn emerged unopposed from the topside accessway of the tunnel complex. He removed the NVGs and flung them aside, no longer needing them in the moonlit darkness of night, in which stars winked overhead and desert sand instead of concrete slabs lay beneath his sneakered feet.

Off to his left he spotted a cluster of shacks, and when he drew nearer, he realized it was the site of one of several ghost towns located in the area. In this case it was the remains of an old gold mining boomtown dating back to the 1890s.

What brought Quinn into the town was the battered pickup truck parked outside a ramshackle structure.

An old man with a gray beard and a straw Stetson perched on his head came from inside and stood in the doorway. Quinn saw that the place had been converted into a small canteen and souvenir shop selling rocks, minerals, postcards and other memorabilia to the tourists who came out from Vegas and Reno.

After a few minutes of negotiation, Quinn had the keys to the pickup and a promise from the old-timer to deny that he'd ever laid eyes on him.

9

Directorate Two-Zero was located in Langley, Virginia, in a wing of the CIA's headquarters building devoted to the activities of the Operations Directorate. Permission to enter the section required the highest security clearance it was possible to obtain. In fact, to most of the rank and file, D-20 did not even officially exist.

That was because Directorate Two-Zero had been created for a single specific purpose. The purpose of the clandestine operations section was to oversee the testing and deployment of the ultrasecret Upcard program.

Cable traffic and incoming reports from assets deployed in the field had made it increasingly clear that the clone bearing the government serial number C.U.-129GR had been released from its neural network cyberpod as part of a concerted effort with precisely calculated ends.

The specifics of those objectives were on the mind of Casper Nordquist, chief of D-20, as he sat poring over computer records with loosened tie and eyes shot through with red from hours of tedious scanning of both paper documents and electronic media.

Seated across from him was his assistant, John Lorimer. The subject under discussion was what to do about the escaped hybrid entity that was more weapon than it was man, more machine than it was flesh and blood.

"We're playing catch-up ball when we should be in the home stretch," Lorimer said. "Every day that Griffin remains free is another day closer to the fire. Then there's the issue of Quinn."

"Yes," Nordquist answered. "I'm well aware of Quinn's role in this boondoggle. And I'm also aware that you might have personal reasons for not wanting Quinn taken out of the running. Your friendship with him doesn't impact on the current situation."

Lorimer poured himself a fresh cup of black coffee from the pot he'd just made to see them through the night's task of crisis management. "My point is that he has a right to be informed of the true specifics of the situation. We can't continue to allow him to be the object of a clandestine termination initiative."

"Why the hell not?" Nordquist shot back at his subordinate. "Do you realize the kind of ass-chewing we'll take if and when the truth of the operation comes out? Quinn would not be the first nor the last pawn to be sacrificed in the name of operational security. Nor would you or I be treated differently if our butts were on the firing line."

"You're misunderstanding my concern. It isn't with policy. It's with *how* policy is being applied *here*. Quinn might be of invaluable assistance. He was selected for Upcard explantation precisely because of his unique capabilities. In light of our current predicament, he might well be the only man on earth capable of assisting us. There's the Bradley Theorem, for example, which states that—"

"Damn it Lorimer," Nordquist cut in, "I know all about what it says about twins, even clonal pairs, being able to intuitively sense what the other is doing, thinking or feeling. Don't think I haven't considered the options," he asserted. "But we haven't talked to the President yet. That's the purpose of our burning the midnight oil tonight—proactive damage control. We've got to be good and sure of our options before we talk to the old man."

"I still think we should call the dogs off Quinn." Lorimer pressed his point. "I maintain that the man holds the crucial key to damage control regarding the unstable cybernetic unit.''

''You're forgetting one critical factor,'' Nordquist said, this time with an ironic smile playing across his gaunt, unshaven features.

''What's that, sir?'' Lorimer asked.

''We don't even know where the hell Quinn is right now.''

HIS FEATURES RIGID with concentration, Griffin scanned the backlit plasma display of the compact palmtop workstation, sitting in the cone of dusty light that filtered through the window of the Los Angeles motel room he had rented.

He had paid for the room with cash instead of plastic and had registered under an assumed name. Voice-stress analysis had assured Griffin that the middle-aged couple behind the desk were not reacting in any unusual manner to his presence. Griffin was certain he was not suspected.

The small but powerful unit was patched through ordinary switched telecommunication lines to an ultrasecret government computer network. The computer code that Griffin had written allowed him to penetrate into the heart of the system.

Accessing the electronic nerve center gave him the ability to stealthily scan the operating system for hidden "doorways" in the software and to enter these with the stealth of a cat burglar and the deadliness of a data virus.

Finding one such doorway and entering it covertly, Griffin was now scanning the vast hypertext database of the National Security Council's Deltax electronic mail system.

Using artificial-intelligence-driven search protocols, the cyborg was probing for information that would help him decide on how to carry out the directive he had received in the cyberpod chamber, which would determine his actions until his mission was accomplished.

It was a termination directive that Griffin had been tasked with carrying out—a hit order on the President.

Griffin had been considering several options toward achieving his assigned objective.

Air Force One, the President's official aircraft, might offer an opportunity to launch a strike against the commander in chief.

The White House itself, though heavily fortified against ground and air assaults, nevertheless had numerous vulnerable points that he could penetrate.

As he continued his scan, one particular database entry in a long column of glowing on-screen listings suddenly jumped out at Griffin.

As Griffin read on, his initial curiosity changed to keen interest, then doubt, and finally became a growing conviction that events would take an entirely different direction than planned as he scrolled through the database entry.

The entry was keyed to other listings in the hypertext-based information storage-and-retrieval architecture. These entries Griffin methodically checked, as well, weighing the startling new possibilities that they had suddenly opened up.

Now Griffin realized beyond a shadow of a doubt that the termination directive—with which he had originally been tasked in the cyberpod through his bioelectronic programming interface—was effectively nullified.

The new information his probe had uncovered made the objective of the mission obsolete. Griffin was now freed from having to carry out the strike.

This meant that the parahuman was free to pursue new ends, ends that he had suddenly realized were now within his power to achieve.

Logging out of the database and making sure to cover his electronic tracks, Griffin punched in a new series of commands.

The Deltax hack had opened his eyes. Griffin now had one final task to perform.

He had a message to deliver to his control.

DEEP WITHIN a building half a world away, in the Moscow headquarters of the Komitet Gosudarstvennoi Bezopasnosti, better known by the acronym KGB, Colonel Sergei Korniyenko sat behind his desk and received the decoded telemetry.

The source of the transmission was the cybernetically enhanced clonal organism referred to by the code name Griffin. The Russian's face betrayed the inner turmoil that made his head throb painfully as he read and reread the transmission with a growing sense of panic.

Though the message was tersely worded, it fully managed to imply that the course of history would be changed in an unexpected and terrifying manner: "All bets are off. ARGUS already operational. Details follow. *Das Vidanya.*"

Korniyenko scanned the documentation provided by Griffin. As he absorbed the material, he knew with a veteran's gut appreciation that there was no faking data of this high a grade and that he was not looking at disinformation.

These data were bona fide, and this fact meant that the entire warp and woof of his elaborately woven scenario would no longer hold together. The American President would live, he knew.

But the world, and mankind along with it, might very well not survive the coming onslaught that he had brought about by releasing the cybernetically augmented clonal entity.

That, however, was no longer Korniyenko's concern. His own death was imminent, only mere minutes away.

With the message he had just received, the Russian realized that his own existence had effectively come to an end. For the crime he had committed against both the Russian people and the human race, there was only a single punishment.

His only options left now, Korniyenko realized, were to inflict it himself or permit others to do it. He chose the former option.

Minutes later Korniyenko's aide in the outer room heard the single shot and immediately ran into the office.

He found Colonel Korniyenko slumped across his desk, a dark stream of blood pouring from the hole in the side of his skull and running down onto the carpeted floor. The pistol was still clutched in his hand, and the office was filled with smoke from the documents Korniyenko had burned just prior to inflicting the final judgment on himself and thereby denying the world its future course of justice.

10

From her fiery core, Nature had forged the mountain from pure iron. Its rocky ferrous mass made it naturally impervious to the ravaging effects of nuclear-blast-generated EMP, or electromagnetic pulse—more so than any man-made structure on the face of the earth.

For this reason, it was the single most important installation for the storage of electronic data of all types in the continental United States. The federal government, along with the governments of most states, cities and municipalities, as well as those of several foreign countries, stored their most vital documents in the Iron Mountain complex in Leeds, Pennsylvania.

Leeds was under federal jurisdiction due to its unparalleled strategic importance. A permanently assigned corps of troops guarded the installation day and night.

The facility's single entrance was heavily fortified, and ingress and egress were tightly restricted.

The safety of Iron Mountain was critical to the security of the nation and the integrity of international monetary exchange. Because of the critical data stored within the repository at Leeds, some claimed that it was the single most important locale on the face of the earth.

THE ARMORED CAR rolled up to the main gate of the high-security installation. Beyond the gate began a four-lane asphalt road.

The road extended straight on for three hundred yards until it was swallowed up by the cavernous mouth of the entrance to the mountain storage complex.

This yawning doorway into the facility could be secured within seconds by an enormous steel blast door that slid down and locked in place, hermetically sealing the base interior from external threats.

The armored vehicle stopped just short of the guard post that was strategically situated at the center of a chain-link security fence forming a three-sided perimeter around the accessway to the Iron Mountain storage depot.

The uniformed driver presented the guard with his manifest, and the uniformed sentinel leafed through the sheaf of printouts. Everything on the manifest appeared to be in order.

According to the documentation presented by the driver, the armored truck bore a cargo of computerized transaction records from a New York City savings-and-loan establishment. The guard's handheld computer confirmed that the delivery of the data was expected at the repository.

As the guard handed the manifest back to the driver, he noticed that the man in the shotgun seat had not moved since the truck had pulled in. He sat with his visored cap pulled low over his face and his chin slung low on the front of his brown uniform.

"Your partner looks tired," the sentry told the driver, curiously eyeing the second man.

"Tired?" the driver replied with a laugh and a conspiratorial wink. "Ray's dead to the world. If you got as lucky as he did last night, you would be, too, believe me."

"Okay," the sentry replied with a smile, understanding the implication of a night of drunken pleasure with a woman. "You're cleared."

"Thanks, partner," returned the driver, flashing him a broad grin. Putting the truck in gear, he began rolling slowly toward the yawning entrance to the cavern complex.

The interior of the area just beyond the entrance was a huge vault, cathedrallike and soaring into the belly of the mountain. Two uniformed sentries armed with M-20 caseless rifles stood guard at either side as the truck rolled toward the mouth of the cavern.

Applying the brakes, the driver slowed the truck to a crawl as he reached the second speed bump and red-and-black-striped trestle barrier. The sentries stationed beyond raised the barrier and waved him through. The driver then steered the truck into the parking area and stepped from the cab.

As he did, Griffin pulled a Minigun M-214 from the seat and flipped on its motor. This Minigun series was a lighter and more compact version of the standard-sized weapon, which fired standard SS109 ammunition. It was designed to be used in the role of a light support weapon.

Easily handheld, it could be deployed to devastating advantage by a single man. Griffin also activated the switch beneath the dashboard, which would detonate the Semtex charge under the front seat and blow up the truck.

Griffin's motions in exiting the vehicle caused the dead second man to topple out of the door onto the asphalt, where he lay sprawled with his legs in the truck and his torso on the black mac-adam. It was immediately noticed by one of the sentries but still too late for his own good.

"Hey, you!" he shouted at Griffin. "What the hell's going on?"

Griffin triggered the Minigun in answer to the guard's shouted question. It cycled out its 5.56 mm steeljackets at a blinding rate of fire. The impact of scores of bullets tore hunks out of the sentry's face and torso. His entire body shook and jittered under the impact as splatters of blood and pulverized organ matter jumped from every inch of his body.

As the first takedown collapsed, the second sentry was cut down by another fusillade a few moments later as he managed to bring his M-20 assault weapon into play and got off a burst of caseless ammo.

Alarm sirens were already sounding as Griffin pivoted on his heels and strode toward a cham-ber located lateral to the main bay, where a huge service elevator giving access down to the lower levels of the base was situated.

The immense blast door of the facility was closing, too, throwing a dark shadow over the interior bay. Reaching the elevator, Griffin pushed one of the two panel buttons, and the large stainless-steel doors slid quickly open.

Griffin stepped into the car just as a contingent of soldiers was hotfooting it toward his position, their shouts drowned out by the nonstop noise of alarm sirens.

Inside the armored truck by which Griffin had gained access to the base, the LCD of the charge timer showed a column of glowing red zeros. In a heartbeat the Semtex charge detonated with an earsplitting report. The explosion tore the truck to pieces in a yellow-black fireball.

Troops arriving on the scene were bowled over by the concussive force of the immensely powerful blast waves cycling from the explosion's epicenter.

Griffin rode the utility elevator down three levels, to the deepest node of the sprawling storage facility, which extended through the heart of the mountain like burrows made by enormous termites.

When the doors of the elevator opened sometime later, Griffin found himself face-to-face with a contingent of uniformed, helmeted soldiers. They were armed with high-capacity light support weapons firing caseless ammo tipped with explosive heads.

Griffin opened up with the Minigun as the opposition began firing. The rounds that struck his armored glacis exploded harmlessly as they punched through the layer of flesh covering the surgically implanted steel skeletal understructure.

Before any more rounds could strike one of the critical areas not protected by the steel implants, Griffin launched a long, chattering burst of 5.56 mm steel at the troopers, mowing down those in the front ranks like stalks of wheat before the Reaper's scythe.

The base personnel at the rear got off dozens of rounds. It did them little good, however. They were astounded to see the rips appearing in the intruder's brown uniform but no blood issue from the mangled flesh beneath the rent fabric. Pieces of Griffin's face were shot away, too, exposing the dull glint of metal beneath, and the survivors' terror was complete.

"Sweet Jesus! It's a robot!" one of them shouted, and pitched a grenade at Griffin. Reacting with speed no ordinary man could match, Griffin caught the grenade in one hand and hurled it back at the base defenders, all in the space of the fleeting seconds left before the submunition detonated.

The grenade fragmented an instant after the toss, catapulting the last remaining soldiers into the walls, their arms and legs sheared off by the exploding front of razor-edged shrapnel.

Now Griffin continued on toward the objective that had brought him to Leeds.

Superimposed over the corridor through which he strode, he could see a flashing yellow square indicating the position of the specific room in the sublevel—his destination.

Griffin reached this destination minutes later.

A heavy steel door barred access to this storage vault. Griffin dealt with the door by punching a hole in it, then pulling it off its heavy-duty hinges.

Stepping into the room beyond, he looked around while his surgically implanted processors analyzed the visual data.

The chamber contained a computer terminal. The cases of computer disks were stacked on shelves along the walls and arranged in rows throughout the room.

Griffin stepped quickly to the computer terminal and began inputting a series of coded search protocols with a speed no other human on earth could duplicate.

In seconds the data readout appearing on the screen told Griffin which specific disk he was looking for. He reached inside his brown guard's uniform and produced a plastic disk case containing a silvery compact disk which was identical to the thousands of cases lining the shelves of the enormous room.

Moving quickly, he substituted the disk case beneath his uniform jacket for another one from the shelves. Griffin then logged off the computer screen and exited the storage chamber.

He reached the end of the corridor just as a heavy metal bulkhead was closing in front of him. As it slid shut, cylindrical black grenades bounced beneath the closing metal shield. Before Griffin could reach the shield, the grenades went off, releasing fast-rising clouds of dense, choking gas.

Beyond the two-inch-thick blast door, the leader of the strike detail consulted his watch. The T7 nerve agent was highly lethal and it acted quickly. After several minutes he instructed his men to don their gas masks and ordered the blast shield raised again.

They found Griffin still standing on the other side. All at once the Minigun M-214 in his hands blazed out its shattering knell.

Cutting the opposition down as they fired their weapons at him, Griffin strode through the decimated ranks amid clouds of choking cordite smoke and rivulets of hot blood and was quickly lost around the bend in the corridor.

Proceeding with great speed, Griffin next found the ventilation grating he was looking for. Ripping it from its niche in the wall, he crawled into the shaft beyond. The glowing green icons and pop-up text boxes visible as an overlay on his visual field showed him the precise branches to take toward safety.

He moved through the duct system at tremendous speed, following his IVD's electronic route map. Minutes later he was punching his way through a steel bulkhead and heaving himself through the mouth of a maintenance shaft terminating on the side of the mountain.

Moving down the slope at speeds no ordinary human was capable of reaching, Griffin soon found the small helicopter that he had landed hours before. It had been hidden behind a radar-absorbent camouflage tarp whose "smart" skin network of LCD nodes continuously painted its surface with an image of the background environment, making it a virtual cloak of invisibility.

Stripping off the camo tarp, Griffin climbed behind the copter's controls and lifted the bird from the LZ.

Flying nap of the earth to evade ground radar, he was far from the scene of the strike in minutes, totally lost to the search parties sent out after him.

11

Rain came down in cold, gray, whipping sheets as Quinn pulled the beat-up '93 TransAm into the parking area of a deserted strip mall. The old car was faster than appearances might indicate, though. He'd bought the vehicle in Ketchum, Idaho, taking care to select a garage that was also a custom shop.

The car had been customized to Quinn's exact specifications, and it had cost him plenty, especially when the mechanic began to suspect that Quinn was running from something or somebody. There were 490 horses under the hood, a Cyclone exhaust system, a Hurst Strato-Matic four-on-the-floor and a custom-installed, electronically self-calibrating Hays clutch.

Apart from the fact that it was two-thirty in the morning, a chain of heavy thunderstorms had kept the Illinois highway clear of traffic and the streets of Cahokia devoid of pedestrians.

Quinn was tired to the bone. He had been on the run for weeks, living off the contents of the money belt stuffed with hard cash he'd drawn by wire transfer from a numbered offshore contingency account he kept for emergencies—his "spooker," as it would have been called in his old covert days.

The spooker would hold out for a long while yet, but running had been taking its toll on him psychologically, as well as physically.

From Ketchum to Kansas City, Quinn had played computer cracker with the U.S. government's most well guarded database networks. Neither electronic nor print media had carried a word about the ongoing manhunt that had the man called Nomad as its target.

To Quinn this fact alone spoke volumes about a spook operation. What's more, the mere fact that such a tight lid had been successfully maintained on a search of such magnitude was in itself a strong indication that it was sanctioned at the highest operational levels.

Still more revealing to Quinn was the fact that his series of computer penetrations was met by repeated security measures. The Intelligence agencies and knowledge banks of the federal government, and even the private sector to some extent, had apparently been quietly placed on alert for cracking attempts.

Was it because those who hunted Quinn were aware that his logical search for a reason behind the hunt lay in the electronic storehouse of computerized records? Or did this mean that another cracker had penetrated security-coded files simultaneously with Quinn?

Quinn had learned this much, though. A code name had continually cropped up in the stream of raw data through which he sifted like a miner searching for nuggets of gold: Upcard.

His probe had revealed that in the past weeks there had been a great deal of curiosity and consternation regarding Upcard from every echelon of the Intelligence community.

Throughout the hidden corridors of power, which were the true centers of history and politics and spelled life and death for the millions who believed that they had the freedom to control their destinies, there came the smell of fear.

Security had been breached, and a weapon that they had been assured would never see the light of day was missing.

Much of the electronic traffic regarding Upcard had come from Agency sources, and Quinn had gleaned that Maggard, one of the men who had taken him from Tahoe to the Vegas euthanasia center, had been a CIA field asset.

Quinn's instincts told him that he was the center of another of the Company's botched operations. He was the possible object of a massive, far-reaching cover-up, the combined pointman and fall guy of a clandestine fuckup of cosmic proportions.

He would not be the first or the last to be singled out by the Intelligence bureaucracy to cover its operational mistakes. But he wasn't prepared to sit back and let himself be used by the spooks as an officially sanctioned whipping post.

What Quinn planned now was a long shot, but it was the only potential source of critically needed information: Quinn needed a bridge between the Company and himself.

John Lorimer's name had cropped up in several coded reports Nomad had scanned during his cracking activities. Lorimer had been a CIA liaison who was part of the Intelligence support activity for the elite counterterror agency known as Scepter years before. Quinn had gotten to know Lorimer and had liked the man, who had shown more integrity than most others he'd met in the Intelligence arena.

Quinn decided he would attempt to contact Lorimer. It was a strategy of last resort, but it was the only initiative he could come up with at the moment that seemed to present any hope of success.

The cold rain was falling harder and steadier as Quinn climbed out of the car and walked the few feet to a three-phone kiosk on the fringe of the parking area.

He consulted his wrist chronometer. The LCD readout gave him the time: 02:43 a.m. If his gambit had proven successful, the phone should ring in precisely two minutes' time.

If the phone did not ring, then the speed of the turbocharged TransAm would be of critical importance. Failure of the phone to ring would mean Quinn had been compromised by the hunters and had to get out of the area quickly, or he would die.

The phone rang at precisely 2:45. Quinn snatched the handset from its cradle on the first shrill beep. The voice on the other end of the line addressed him by name.

"Quinn, are you there? It's Lorimer."

The voice did not sound like that of a man recently awakened from sleep. Quinn had not believed that it would; Lorimer would have been working late hours if the data intercepts he'd read were accurate.

Quinn paused a beat before responding, checking the LCD readout of the portable voice-stress analyzer coupled to the mouthpiece and assuring himself that it gave him a clean reading before answering.

"I want you to listen carefully, Lorimer," Quinn replied. "There's no way you can trace this call in time to get a fix on my position, so don't even try."

The original call placed to Langley had been initiated by a computer in a motel room in Fairbank, Iowa, hundreds of miles from Quinn's present location.

The number given by the voice-mail unit, in turn, was only the first in a series of rooms with call-forwarding units connected to the phones.

At the end of the chain of electronic Chinese-puzzle boxes was the phone booth in Illinois, but it would be a chain that the Company, despite all its resources, could not trace before Quinn could be miles from the scene.

"Of course you know we're trying right now," Lorimer said back. Beside him, listening in on a second line, was Casper Nordquist. Lorimer was sitting in the director's office, his desk littered with empty coffee cups. "Without much success, though."

"And you won't have any," Quinn affirmed. "Lorimer, I'm tired of running. I don't have to tell you what you already know—you spooks set me up. I want the termination directive cancelled. I want to know the full details of whatever operation I've become involved in. And, Lorimer, I want it *now.*"

"Or what, Quinn? You haven't told me what you'd do if these conditions weren't satisfied."

"I don't have much, but enough to go public with. It's not hard to do."

In the office at Langley, Lorimer looked over at Nordquist, who nodded at him as he lit up a noncarc cigarette and drew the menthol smoke deep into his lungs.

"Okay," he said. "You've got what you want. In fact, we've got some problems of our own you might be able to help us with."

"The Gateway Arch," Quinn told Lorimer. "North end of the park grounds. Two hours from now."

"That's impossible!" Lorimer grated in response. "I'm in D.C. right now. There's just not enough lead time to allow me to make the meet in St. Louis."

"Two hours. *Be there,*" Quinn repeated, and racked the phone. Lorimer would come. Quinn knew that he would.

In the director's office Lorimer let the handset fall to the cradle, where it clattered into place with a hollow sound that echoed the emptiness he felt in his sleep-deprived brain.

Nordquist had already punched in commands for hard copy of the data recorded by the automatic line trace, complete with voice-stress analysis, although the veteran Intelligence officer knew that Quinn's statement was no idle boast—the call would almost certainly prove untraceable.

From all indicators, it looked as though Quinn was telling the truth.

The call had been routed twice before the trail went cold, the trace revealed. It could take days before the termination point could be conclusively discovered, even with the most sophisticated methods available.

"He's a smart son of a bitch," Nordquist said, stubbing out his cigarette in the ashtray on the gunmetal desk. "You'd better get going."

12

The Gateway Memorial Park in St. Louis was deserted as Quinn carefully watched Lorimer approach from the direction of the six-hundred-thirty-foot-high steel arch whose silvery span was now cut off from view by a layer of dark gray clouds.

The storm that had started earlier that morning and had reached Quinn miles away had worsened by now. Cold sheets of rain were still falling steadily, with no sign of letup in sight.

The two men faced each other in the dank cold of early morning, Lorimer in a belted raincoat and Quinn in a weatherized parka, his hand never far from the speed rig that housed the P-90 CAW, which had a round already chambered and forty-nine more in the clear plastic mag that lay horizontally across the weapon's receiver.

From his position Quinn had a clear vantage point from which he could gain advance warning of anyone approaching the meeting place.

Lorimer was a little older than Quinn had remembered, but otherwise the Intelligence agent looked about the same, with a youthful face and lank brown hair that fell across his forehead in a haphazard sweep.

It was an appearance that belied a sharp mind and was deliberately cultivated to conceal a ruthless veteran's skill in the complexities of covert tradecraft.

"I want you to know something right off the bat," Lorimer told Quinn. "I was opposed to what went down from the first."

"Then I *was* set up," Quinn ventured, never letting his eyes stay on Lorimer's longer than a second before he again scanned the surrounding area.

Lorimer nodded affirmatively. "You were set up. Actually you were set up in the name of operational purity. The brass hats are like the Inquisition in the middle ages. You fit the heretic mold, Quinn, and it almost got you crucified. You did right by contacting me. I can help. I *want* to help."

"Then fill me in. I want to know as much as you can tell me. And I want to know it quickly."

"There was an escape from a high-security penal facility," Lorimer began. "The killer went on a homicidal rampage. You were identified as the escapee."

"I was *what?*" Quinn blurted out in shock and disbelief. "How could that be?"

"It could. It was. I repeat, you were identified as the escapee," Lorimer continued, looking a little sheepish. "It's not so surprising, given the fact that the individual we're after both resembles you closely enough to be your twin brother and has no record whatsoever concerning his own existence."

"You've lost me, Lorimer," Quinn spoke out in astonishment. "Stop talking in circles. Clarify."

"We suspect you've penetrated some high-security databases, Quinn," Lorimer continued, prefacing his coming remarks. "In doing so, you've learned about Upcard. The individual who's been doing the damage is a product of Upcard's advanced technology. He is a cybernetic organism, or cyborg, a human clone augmented with sophisticated bioengineering. But more to the point, Quinn, he is *your* clone."

"My *what!*" Quinn rasped. "How? How in the name of—"

"Upcard was a Company project in conjunction with DARPA—Defense Advanced Research Programs Agency—to develop a soldier suited to what was then foreseen as the coming nuclear-biological battlefield,'' Lorimer went on, preventing Quinn from interrupting with a wave of his hand.

"We had known the Soviets to be working along similar lines for decades. This was a game of catch-up ball and desperately needed for the sake of national security. The subjects were Special Forces personnel, selected for their fighting abilities. Explantations of skin tissue were taken covertly, during routine medical exams. Your clone made all the others look like amateurs,'' he concluded with the hint of a smile.

"You son of a bitch,'' Quinn said softly in a knife-edged rasp. "You and all the other self-righteous scumbags in the Company. You cloned me? Without my consent. And now your Frankenstein monster is on the loose. And now you want to hunt me down in its place.''

"In a nutshell, yes,'' Lorimer returned. "Except that there is more to the situation than these facts alone might imply. We believe that the clone was deliberately freed to pursue a secret agenda. One which—''

Quinn suddenly tensed as his hand moved under the parka and closed around the plastic handgrip of the CAW. Out of the corner of his eye he now detected signs of movement, originating in the fringe of trees growing at the perimeter of the park grounds.

Lorimer had seen this, too, and knew what it meant: the presence of killers in the rain. Killers who were coming to exterminate him.

Company killers.

"You won't walk away if I go down," Quinn snarled at Lorimer. With a rasp of Velcro fastenings torn apart, the advanced-design weapon bulked dangerously in his hand. The P-90 CAW was now aimed at Lorimer's heart. A 5.70 mm round already sat in the chamber, ready for firing.

"Believe me, Quinn," Lorimer shouted above the pops of sudden automatic fire. "I had no idea. This was done without my knowledge."

Quinn studied the younger man's face. Despite the front of guilelessness that Quinn knew masked the field operative's keen tactical mind, Quinn saw in his eyes that he was telling the truth. But the autofire had intensified by now, and Quinn had to move fast or lose the moment.

"Quinn," Lorimer told him. "Let me talk to them. Let me—"

Boooooooom!

The resounding clamor of multiple-phased explosions echoed through the rainswept dawn as the automatic firing suddenly stopped.

Taking its place were the sudden screams of wounded men and the frantic shouts of the confused human wolves who had just lost the initiative of their surprise attack.

Anticipating a double cross on the part of the spooks, Quinn had planted a cordon of C-4 antipersonnel charges in a semicircle around the meeting ground.

There was only one corridor out of the semicircle of death. Quinn now pushed Lorimer toward that corridor of safety.

More phased explosions followed in rapid succession as the two men ran through the steadily falling sheets of ice-cold rain over the park's sodden grass. In the distance Quinn heard shouts of *"They're getting away!"* and curses of consternation from the thwarted strikers.

The spooks were trapped within the circle of antipersonnel explosions and pinwheeling shrapnel. Completely disoriented by the effectiveness of Quinn's countermeasure, they fired their weapons through the pall of smoke but were unable to sight on their escaping quarry.

Minutes later Quinn and Lorimer emerged onto a street located near the grounds where Quinn had parked his car. Quinn got into the car, disabled the antitheft fléchette charge that would fire a metal bolt into a car booster's midsection, and turned to face the Company agent.

"You get back to Langley," he told Lorimer. "You deliver my terms to your boss. I'll be in touch."

Lorimer straightened up and watched as the TransAm screamed away into the rainy post-dawn twilight, hearing the shouts of the mauled hunters drawing nearer as the survivors of the failed ambush began emerging from the cordon of death.

13

A glance in the camera-linked, zoom-capable rearview mirror showed the chase cars fishtailing into the lane behind him as Quinn careered the TransAm onto the rain-slicked highway.

It was early morning, hours yet before rush-hour traffic would clog the beltway that looped around the urban hub of downtown St. Louis, skirting the Mississippi riverfront for most of its length before it swung back into the outlying bedroom communities.

Three cars had appeared in the rearview—large sedans with powerful air-cooled engines.

In the rearview Quinn saw one vehicle pull ahead of the other two. A figure on the passenger side stuck his arm out the window.

He clutched something boxy and black in his fist.

A moment later tongues of fire pulsed from its conical tip, and Quinn heard bullets thunk against the rear fender of his speed car.

Backup had been expected.

Quinn was ready.

The TransAm had been customized to blow the doors off anything on the roads. Now, as it ate up the highway under triple-tread mag tires, Quinn was confident that his street machine would perform as expected.

Quinn had not been idle in the hours before setting up the meet, nor had the ring of antipersonnel mines he'd seeded on the Gateway Arch grounds been the only surprise he'd planned for any pursuit teams that might cross his path.

Across the bridge that spanned the Mississippi, across the state line in Illinois, lay the sister city of East St. Louis. Quinn had chosen the Gateway Arch site with the peculiar conjunction of these two cities in mind.

Nowhere else in the continental U.S. did such a municipal arrangement exist. East St. Louis was smaller than the metropolis across the river to its west, and its waterfront zone was a warren of warehouses and aimlessly meandering streets, unlike the largely renovated waterfront of St. Louis itself.

Quinn had spent the better part of the past twenty-four hours in East St. Louis preparing a getaway route in the event that he would be pursued by the spooks or whoever else might get in his way.

Now Quinn roared across the highway, drawing the chase crews into some big trouble if they were intent on following him.

With its powerful, electronically controlled, fuel-injected V-8 engine, the TransAm was able to stay well ahead of the chase vehicles, and its bulletproof glass and rear blast shield afforded protection against their automatic-weapons fire.

Quinn could see the bridge looming up ahead through dense fog shrouding the riverfront as he savagely wrenched the steering wheel to take the bridge on-ramp at eighty-five miles per hour.

Double-shifting the Hurst, pushing the stick forward while stomping down on the clutch, he roared across the bridge and reached East St. Louis a few minutes later, the TransAm's heavy-duty shocks and oversize springs taking the bumps in the road without a single hitch.

Suddenly a burst of steeljacketed tens struck his rear tires. The hit would have sent any other vehicle moving as fast as Quinn's was into a terminal spin. But the tires were the run-flat kind, their centers filled with a silicon-based plastic filler, and the vehicle's progress was unaffected.

Mashing down his foot on the gas pedal, Quinn poured on still more speed despite the heavy fire being launched toward him by the hit crews in the chase vehicles close behind him.

"Damn it, can't we catch the guy?" one of the spook paramilitaries in the lead chase car yelled at the wheelman.

"Negative, he's too damn fast," the wheelman responded with a grimace.

"This is bullshit! I'm calling in air support," the second man said, putting a compact commo unit to his lips and speaking rapidly as they bumped along. "Magic Able to Gallant Echo. Mobilize the chopper, we're getting nowhere fast this way."

"Roger," the crisp, no-sweat tones of a professional came back. "Copter support is on the way. Over."

"Backup's coming," the guy in the shotgun seat said to the man behind the wheel, palming a second clip of 10 mm rounds into the SMG. "Just try to stay on his back. If we can't go for a kill, then maybe we can spot for the chopper. It *will* take care of him."

Meanwhile, the TransAm had gone bouncing over the far side of the bridge, its undercarriage thudding and scraping across the grooves of the striated metal road surface as the chopper lifted off from its LZ two miles away and set a course to its strike coordinates.

Strapped into the catbird seat, feeling every vibration of the airframe as the instrument panels glowed green and both engines growled with mechanical life, the sky jockey felt as though he were part man, part machine, a godlike chimera poised to hurl jagged bolts of lightning at his target below.

The flyboy pulled on his sidearm controller and collective pitch stick, and the rotorcraft rose effortlessly into the air. Banking sharply, he slewed laterally across the river through the dense fog of the storm-lashed city, his electronic eyes peering through the mist as his navigational system helped him with computer-driven speed and precision.

By now Quinn had reached the outskirts of the warren of streets that twisted and snaked without rhyme or reason into the industrial-waterfront district over the state line in East St. Louis.

Displayed in his rearview mirror, Quinn saw the chase cars still behind him in the diminishing rain, his speed and driving skill combining to make him an unattainable target.

Now he would shift from defensive to offensive tactics.

Now it was his turn to strike.

Flipping on the TransAm's dash-mounted GPS unit, with its preprogrammed map coordinates, Quinn watched the supertwist plasma screen beside the steering column wink to life, the grid of the waterfront district's streets traced by a flashing broken line in electronic blue, which demarcated the route Quinn was to follow.

Flashing circles here and there along the street grid indicated several locations in the industrial zone where Quinn had placed vicious surprises for each of the chase cars.

Cornering tightly, Quinn swung the high-performance vehicle into a narrow street where the thin asphalt cover had weathered away to expose the original nineteenth-century paving cobbles.

As Quinn spotted the lead chase car again in the rearview, he hit one of the buttons on the dash console punch pad.

The first glowing circle on the GPS immediately winked out, and the console emitted a shrill beep. A glance at the mirror in wide-angle mode, and Quinn saw the first chase car pop into view, followed by the second car a moment later.

Not so with the third car.

The earsplitting blast of a powerful explosion echoed across the rainswept streets as it was caught in the first of the Hogan's Alley traps Quinn had rigged, this one a variation on the "tank breaker."

The explosive charge blew away a wooden holdback beam keeping in place a two-ton steel I-beam that hung from a rooftop by a twenty-foot steel cable. Welded to the I-beam's front was a four-foot metal spike.

As the I-beam swung free, the spike on its end smashed with brutal force into the chase car's windshield, impaling the driver through the upper abdomen like an insect on a pin as he screamed in agony and thrashed about in the grip of a howling madness that immediately preceded his death.

The impaled wheelman's hot blood drenched the shooter sitting to his right as it splashed across the shattered windshield while angular momentum sent the car crashing into a building wall.

In moments the gas tank caught fire, and the car was soon reduced to a charred, blackened wreck amid a roiling mass of flames belching skyward and giving off a rising column of thick, stinking smoke.

Quinn wrenched the steering wheel and hung a series of tight lefts and rights, following the route highlighted on his GPS. The surviving two chase vehicles were still on him, intent on pursuit.

The second Hogan's Alley was coming up fast on his left, according to the dash-mounted GPS.

This death trap was located in a narrow alley between rows of long-ago abandoned industrial buildings. Quinn roared down the length of the alley, pursued by the two chase vehicles that remained.

A battery of multiple-grenade launchers he'd placed along the walls opened up with another touch on the dashboard control panel, peppering the chase cars with high-explosive canisters. The first car was broadsided at once and immediately went out of control.

Swerving crazily on the rain-slicked pavement, the stricken vehicle flipped over on its side and went skidding into the wall of an adjacent building. Impact was followed by a deafening bang, and the car went up in a roiling fireball that mushroomed into the sky.

Quinn found the third chase car harder to take out of the running than the first two. The next Hogan's Alley had a deadfall trap acting as its killing mechanism. Tons of rubble secured in rope netting was hanging from steel cables straddling the alley across the sides of buildings, ready to be released with crushing force.

But the third car evaded the cascading rain of death as Quinn's TransAm screamed past the trap site. Quinn surmised that the driver of the third car was probably a lot better or a lot more scared than the gung-ho drivers of the other two kayoed cars.

There was a final trap coming up, however, and Quinn swerved into it.

The car followed right along as Quinn made a sudden sharp turn to the right into a narrow alley a split second ahead of the other vehicle.

Overshooting the alley with the screech of tortured rubber as the driver applied his brakes, the chase car plowed into the black tarp that concealed the huge crater in the street and nose-dived into the pit beneath. At the bottom of the pit was a spring-loaded plunger calibrated to set off a pipe bomb containing several pounds of plastic explosive.

The front end of the vehicle crashed headlong into the plunger-detonator as both passenger and driver were thrown through the windshield headfirst.

The titanic force of the explosion of the pipe bomb threw the two-ton vehicle back into the air, spitting it up like a burning stone from a fiery mouth while the blast's thunderous report echoed across the forlorn section of gray, derelict buildings.

The car crashed back to the street as its carburetor exploded and blasted its hood clean off its steel hinges. The burning fuel pump set off the gas in the tank, which blew hunks of the rear end into the air and threw up an incandescent ball of fire.

Quinn pulled the TransAm to a stop and backed to the alley entrance. It was over, he thought as he saw the burning wreckage, but the next minute an earsplitting impact rent the air.

The Hydra missile walloped into the asphalt, perilously close to the side of the car. Quinn's self-sealing gas tank saved him from destruction as hot shrapnel pierced the TransAm's armored carriage. He leaped from the doomed vehicle just as a second heat-seeking missile from the Commanche chopper slammed into the street machine, blowing it into a thousand flaming pieces.

Quinn dived for cover as he heard the sound of the Commanche's engines roaring above the boom of successive explosions.

Now 35 mm chain gun fire raked the street, and Quinn dashed for the protection of a metal Dumpster. From there he struggled under a concrete trestle bridge where trucks were parked with the 35 mm rounds slamming into the asphalt at his heels.

A little farther along the parking area beneath the trestle bridge, Quinn came to the locked steel door of a factory building. After blowing the door with a grenade, he darted inside.

The armored black dragonfly hovered over the factory's roof, looking every bit as lethal as it was. The pilot of the advanced-design assault chopper radioed for a mobile force of paracommandos to take out the fleeing quarry who was trapped in the building.

Quinn was as good as dead.

14

The squat metal cylinder emitted a series of whirrs and clicks as it rolled up to Quinn. The hemispherical turret at its apex bristled with sonic and visual sensors.

The black barrel of an SMG jutting at Quinn from the turret made it plain that the securobot was a lot more dangerous than it appeared at first glance.

"Warning—you have intruded on a private facility," an electronic voice pealed from a speaker grille. "Police have been notified. Do not move. This unit is authorized to employ lethal force if necessary, pursuant to State of Illinois legal code section 7897-B, paragraph 7."

Despite the almost comical appearance of the squat robot security unit, Quinn entertained no illusions as to the deadliness of its sensor-targeted SMG or to the intentions of those who had designed and constructed it.

The question was how far would Quinn have to go before the securobot fired? How tight were the kill parameters? Quinn had to find out in a hurry because he would soon have lethal company—human killers who would have no built-in checks against blowing him away the moment they acquired him in their gunsights.

Quinn tested out the securobot by making a sudden lateral move. Its sensor turret tracked him instantly, but the SMG remained inactive. Quinn jinked sideways once more, now in the opposite direction. Again the securobot tracked him but did not use its SMG.

How much leeway was engineered into the securobot's operating program? Quinn would have to push back the edges of the envelope, which would be a highly risky tactic but no more so in the long run than standing pat and waiting for the chase crew to enter and put him down.

Quinn kept his eyes glued to the deadly turret as he edged closer to a nearby cart bearing mechanical components. When he was a few inches away from the cart, he ducked behind it.

The securobot opened right up with its SMG, but the heavy metal frame of the cart stopped the slugs, which ricocheted harmlessly into the air.

Drawing the P-90, Quinn cranked fire at the robot sentinel, aiming high to hit the sensor turret. The high-energy ammunition fired by the close-assault weapon shattered the sensor nodes to which all on-board offensive systems were linked.

The securobot whirled aimlessly about and launched a salvo of careless rounds into the wall, then flopped over with its wheels spinning uselessly in the air.

Quinn took a look around him.

He was in what appeared to be a fully cybernated manufacturing plant.

On the vast ground level into which he had entered, easily taking up two whole city blocks, robotic construction apparatus was assembling the colossal frameworks of heavy industrial machinery.

As gigantic steel claws handled the immense components with acrobatic skill, laser beams pulsed down from swinging robot arms, spot-welding the seams of chassis destined to become part of high-capacity construction equipment.

Jutting from the periphery of the ceiling of the immense assembly plant were the bulging Plexiglas domes of observation booths from which human monitors could have a bird's-eye view of the manufacturing process taking place below.

Quinn did not notice any sign of human overseers in the booths. The sky suites were dark and all of them seemed empty.

Probably the staff—if there were any staff regularly employed at this automated facility—would arrive for work later in the morning. It was still only a little after sunrise, after all.

Quinn knew that he had to find an escape route out of the building in order to avoid the assault that was imminent.

By entering the building, he had temporarily staved off destruction by the Commanche's rockets and automatic guns. However, he had also trapped himself inside the facility.

It was a sure bet that the helicopter pilot had transmitted a request for assault troops who would soon deploy on site.

Quinn hunted for an exit that would take him out of the facility beyond visual range of the chopper. He searched the ground level of the manufacturing plant and spotted a doorway clearly marked as an emergency street exit.

Quinn moved toward it, but suddenly stopped short as the main doorway blew in behind him and automatic fire lancing down from the sky suites above cut him off. The assault crew had arrived.

"Blackjack to Mother. Have acquired target. Repeat, he's in here," the strike leader spoke into throat commo while the other four blacksuited members of his takedown crew burst in from the street entrance.

Quinn ducked out of the line of fire from above as more attackers arrived on scene. Pivoting quickly, he launched a salvo of 5.70s at the dark mass silhouetted above him, forcing the shooter to hustle back into the interior of the room.

Quinn retreated, dodging the pulsed laser beam of a plasma cutter, which swung to and fro on a giant robot arm in his path. Suddenly two strike commandos appeared on a low catwalk, targeting parabellum bursts in his direction.

Breaking sideways, Quinn returned fire from the cover of some bulky equipment. The targeted striker flailed his arms wildly as he was catapulted from the catwalk to land on a rolling trolley that quickly carried him beneath the beam of a plasma welding torch.

The ultrahot beam of high-voltage ions sliced through his midsection as effortlessly as a butcher's axe through a joint of meat.

Blood began spurting in thick gouts, and foul-smelling mist rose from the screaming, thrashing man as the beam cutter sliced him open. He soon became still as a noxious stench of burnt and cauterized flesh filled the factory.

Uttering a curse, the dead man's partner tracked his weapon, barely able to fight back the nausea that churned in his guts, and fired a volley of fléchette rounds from his bullpup weapon at Quinn. But Quinn ducked back behind cover and returned fire on the fly.

The P-90 burst was accurate: it hammered the shooter across his belly and knocked him straight into a robot hole-puncher—a series of enormous wheels studded with steel teeth.

Long, wickedly sharp spikes—ten inches in length and designed to auger through drop-forged steel plating—riddled his head, sinking into his skull and piercing his brain.

Quinn broke from cover and bolted across the factory floor as two more paramilitaries popped up right behind him. He clambered up a short flight of metal utility stairs onto the low catwalk and fired from a crouch. Quinn's rounds were on target. Taking hits, the two shooters went sprawling into the grinding, clattering machinery behind them to be quickly swallowed up within.

Hurtling down a second flight of metal stairs nearer the exit, Quinn caught sight of yet another striker. Quinn fired before the guy could bring his weapon into play, and the commando went down, catching a spray of studs across his belly.

No longer impeded, Quinn sprinted toward the back door and pushed out into the alley beyond. At once he heard the clatter of the Commanche's five-bladed, bearingless rotors overhead. Quinn knew his escape route was impossibly blocked.

With the chopper still in the zone, small-arms fire wouldn't do him any good. Ducking back inside the factory, Quinn looked around him and saw one of the robot laser welders firing a beam of ruby light at a part passing beneath it.

Sprinting toward the robot welder, Quinn saw that the laser unit was detachable. Battery powered, it held a charge that was constantly replenished by being fitted to a power module in the robot's midsection.

Quinn found the main control console below the catwalk and located the operating screen on the console's VDT that controlled the robot. Using the computerized controls, he was able to engineer a complete shutdown of the robot welder.

He raced back down onto the ground floor again and flipped latches, successfully uncoupling the bulky industrial laser welding gun from the now immobilized robot's grasp.

The LCD readout panel on the laser unit showed that it had a ninety percent charge still left in it. Quinn hoped that this would prove sufficient to do what he needed it to accomplish.

Quinn bolted through the door cradling the heavy laser welding gun in his arms. Up above, the Commanche chopper's tracking computer instantly acquired him.

Automatic fire began to walk his way as Quinn sank to one knee and aimed the laser at the chopper's vulnerable underbelly. Pressing the button on the unit's side, he sent a coherent beam of twenty-megawatt pulsed laser energy spurting through space.

The dashes of brilliant red light punched up into the frame of the hovering gunship. Within the cockpit the pilot clutched at his face. Only a smoking crater remained where his nose and eyes and mouth had once been.

Quinn's next burst put the pilot out of his misery as it scored a direct hit on the chopper's fuel compartment located aft of its stub-wing weapons pylons.

Out of control, the chopper suddenly exploded in midair. What was left of its burning tail assembly fell with a crash onto the rooftop of one of the warehouses fronting the alley. Beyond the rooftop a balloon of yellow flame rose into the air along with the thunderous report of a powerful secondary explosion as the nose assembly wreckage hit the deck.

But only minutes remained before another chopper would be sent in. Quinn knew he had to make tracks fast or risk another encounter that might end very differently.

The Humvee personnel carrier that had brought the commandos was parked nearby.

Quinn checked out the vehicle to ensure that it was not booby trapped and then started it up.

Before long, the Humvee roared through the winding streets of East St. Louis, bringing Quinn out of the search zone before his pursuers realized that he had eluded their dragnet once again.

15

Dressed in a worn and faded pair of bib overalls beneath his checked mackinaw, Director of Central Intelligence Sylvain Covington, known to intimates as "Sly," waded through pig excrement amid several dozen grunting swine.

Looking on while the DCI called out, "here, sooo-eee" and tossed handfuls of cornmeal from a gunnysack into the milling livestock in the pigpen, were Directorate Two-Zero chief Nordquist and his assistant, Agent John Lorimer.

Gifted with an intuitive feel for Intelligence, Covington, the progeny of fifteen generations who had cultivated this land, also had farming in his blood.

On weekends and vacations, and during those times when he grappled with especially difficult problems, Covington returned to his roots in Iowa. Working the spread and tending to his livestock, the director could usually get a handle on slippery issues that had eluded him in his office at Langley.

Nordquist and Lorimer, though, the one a Los Angelino, the other a Chicagoan, both felt somewhat uncomfortable as they stood in the biting wind and watched the DCI feed his pigs.

While Nordquist had been to his boss's farm on two prior occasions and knew of the DCI's penchant for discussing sensitive issues at the farmstead, Lorimer had never been that route before.

Accustomed to the antiseptic corridors of CIA headquarters, more at home in front of a computer than beside Covington's herd of prize Chester Whites, he seemed particularly ill at ease in the rural environment.

Nevertheless, Covington had made it clear to his men that the matter of Upcard needed resolution quickly. The President had personally phoned him to inform the DCI that a briefing on board Air Force One was scheduled for the following day.

Covington knew that he would be faced with some tough questions he had damn well better be capable of answering to the satisfaction of the President.

The President might have the reputation of a chief executive with a hands-on managerial style, but Covington, like other Washington insiders, knew that this was by and large a carefully prop-agated publicity hype.

In reality the President often delegated sensi-tive tasks to subordinates.

He was quick to seize the opportunity to claim credit when the outcome worked in his favor. However, when results were not to his liking, or the political winds blew adversely, then he was equally capable of shifting blame onto the shoulders of whoever it was who had been dele-gated responsibility.

Oversight of the Upcard damage-control op-eration had fallen to Covington. In his role as the Agency's director, it was in his ballpark. Cov-ington had in turn kicked the matter downstairs to Nordquist, who had promised immediate re-sults.

These had not yet been forthcoming. The President would demand explanations, and Covington needed those in a hurry.

On this particular weekend at the farm, the problems were multiple, compounded by the fact that Nordquist's department had been making little progress in apprehending the escaped para-human or determining the reasons for Griffin's release in the first place.

But there was also the matter of ARGUS to contend with. Covington had been opposed to the deployment of ARGUS from the very beginning but had found himself in the minority. Oversight of the vast clandestine project had fallen to the National Security Agency, which claimed primacy of place in the realm of signals Intelligence.

Unknown to the world at large, which knew little of the role of ARGUS to begin with, the system was now fully functional, its phased-array network tracking multiple locations across the globe.

The President would be announcing this development at an upcoming press conference. With Griffin at large, though, Covington could not get over the frightening suspicion that the escape of the clone and the installation of the ARGUS net were somehow interlinked.

Covington's ability to find coherent linkages in the wilderness of mirrors that was the field of Intelligence was telling him that the world stood on the brink of a disaster of incalculable magnitude if Griffin remained at large much longer.

Covington emptied the sack of meal and stepped gingerly through the mass of contentedly grunting Chester White hogs toward the gate of the pigsty and let himself out. "Let's walk over there," he said, indicating a barren field where broom corn had grown tall that summer.

Nordquist and Lorimer followed Covington out to the now fallow cornfield, the high rubber boots he'd provided them with becoming spattered with mud from the melted snow of the previous day. As they walked, hearing the wind cutting across the empty field, Covington began sounding out his guests on the matters at hand.

"Your progress report was not encouraging," Covington said to Nordquist. "The President will want to be assured—and I mean completely assured—that Griffin is back in custody or destroyed. So far we've been able to hold the media at bay in the interests of national security, but that ploy won't buy us much more time."

"Griffin is resourceful," Nordquist put in. "He's evaded our dragnet entirely. As for Quinn, he also slipped through the net in St. Louis."

"Sir," Lorimer broke in, "I want to interject that I was and still am opposed to Quinn's being set up as a surrogate target. Griffin should be our only priority. Quinn is not directly involved, and should he contact the media, certain of the disclosures he might make could prove highly embarrassing, to say the least."

"All the more reason to conclude this business before such a contingency materializes," Nordquist said to the younger man. "As far as right and wrong," he went on, "there is a pressing need to contain this event before it becomes public, despite who we have to throw to the dogs. Need I elaborate?"

Covington held up his hand. "Griffin is not only a clonal copy of Quinn, but one that this agency, in conjunction with DARPA, has seen fit to surgically augment with titanium-steel alloy over sixty percent of his body mass.

"We have coupled both eyes to holographic infrared sensors and replaced the bones of his arms and legs with artificial robotic limbs powerful enough to punch through plate steel. We have cut away centers of his brain to make room for a battle-management computer chip more powerful than those on board a B-3 bomber. Just what the hell do you think the media will do with that?"

"The point, Sly, is that the media will never learn the complete story," Nordquist returned. "Griffin, for all his abilities, is only one man acting on his own hook. The combined resources of this and other agencies have been mobilized to apprehend him. He can't stay out in the cold forever. Nobody can."

"You're a fool if you believe that Griffin can't hold out for an indefinite period. Have you forgotten what we created him for?" Covington shot back. "The perfect soldier, a cybernetically enhanced fighting organism who can remain undetected for months, even years, then strike the enemy without warning. We programmed Griffin with all the tools necessary to evade us, and he can keep right on doing that for as long as he likes. Why is he doing it, Nordquist? *What* is his objective?"

"We don't know for sure, but the consensus among the analysts in my section is that Griffin's escape and ARGUS are *not* linked. Due to the very nature of ARGUS and what it implies for the continued existence of the human race if its threat-recognition parameters are violated, there could, after all, be no possible reason why those responsible for Griffin's release would wish him to do anything to trigger ARGUS."

Covington fell silent. Stooping, he picked up a clod of earth and rubbed it between his fingers. Cold and barren now, it nevertheless contained all the nutrients necessary to bring forth a healthy crop come spring. He looked at the two

Intelligence agents and then at the earth in his hands as he collected his thoughts for a few seconds before responding.

"This soil has been farmed by my family for almost a century," he began. "Out here the elements teach us farm people hard lessons, essential truths. One of these is that you take nothing for granted. You never hedge your bets and you never do a half-assed job.

"Unlike you, Nordquist, I cannot ignore the possibility that Griffin is acting autonomously with a specific end in sight. Why not? He's smart enough and capable enough. And if he does have an agenda of his own, I have to ask myself this question—where does the rest of humanity fit in? So far, I haven't been able to answer that question reassuringly."

The director wiped the soil from his hands. Nordquist was unable to reply to what Covington had just told him. But Lorimer already had an answer on the tip of his tongue.

"Humanity wouldn't fit in anywhere, sir. Which is why we need to craft other methods of dealing with Griffin. Before Griffin deals permanently with *us*."

16

From Fort Myers it wasn't far to Cape Coral. The former was what Quinn's old buddy, Cisco Rodriguez, a half-Seminole Indian, had called home after he'd left the world of covert paramilitary operations and retired to the Everglades to earn a living hunting crocodiles. The latter place was where discreet inquiries had revealed to Quinn that Rodriguez now might be found.

Quinn angle-parked the rental car between the two blue stripes on the black asphalt of the parking lot, got out and stepped into the airconditioned coolness of the restaurant, which a pink neon sign in its window identified as Rico and Enrico's Place.

It was before regular hours, and the establishment's tables and chairs were stacked against the walls, the recently mopped floor still showing patches of wetness.

Only the bartender seemed to be around, a scruffy-looking droopy-faced bald guy who was giving glasses halfhearted wipes with his apron.

"We're closed," the bartender said, eyeing Quinn with a look that communicated a cross between challenge and complete apathy.

Quinn walked up to the bar and took a seat on one of the stools that was directly across from where the bartender stood behind the counter.

"Yeah, I know you're closed," he told the basset-faced man, looking him directly in the eyes. "I'm looking for an old buddy of mine. I hear he comes in here a lot. His name's Rodriguez, Cisco Rodriguez."

"Sorry, chief. Don't know nobody named Rodriguez," the bartender replied, looking away from Quinn. "Try Biff's joint down the road. Maybe they can help you."

Quinn laid a fifty-dollar bill down on the bloodred leather counter of the bar. He placed another fifty on top of the first one. He held yet another in his hand.

The bartender tried to look nonchalant, but he was a poor actor. His eyes darted from the bills to Quinn's face and back again, small dark fish unsure of whether or not to snap at the bait dangling so tantalizingly near.

"Think hard," Quinn told him, the last fifty poised in his hand. "It might come to you."

"This guy you mean," the bartender responded, licking his lips, "you ain't got a beef with him or anything like that?"

"Nothing like that," Quinn responded.

"You ain't a cop, right?" the bartender went on, his hand now inching toward the stack of bills.

"Uh-uh," said Quinn, placing the third fifty down on top of the two he'd already laid down on the bar. "No more playing Twenty Questions. Do you know the man I want or not?"

"Guy by the name of Rodriguez's out back," the bartender told Quinn, quickly pocketing the greenbacks. "I don't know if he's the same dude you want. Don't blame me if he ain't."

"Don't worry," Quinn answered. "I won't."

From the rear door a short walk past an open-air eating area filled with vacant tables brought Quinn to a small dry dock where boats were put up on chocks for repairs and cleaning.

Stripped to the waist, a man wearing a red bandanna—tied around his head pirate fashion—and bearing a variety of tattoos on his thickly muscled arms was working on a cabin cruiser supported on a steel framework.

Quinn recognized Rodriguez immediately. So absorbed was he in carefully brushing on a fresh coat of white paint that he apparently didn't notice Quinn stealing up behind him.

"Vatican graffiti squad," Quinn growled. "You're coming with me to whitewash the Sistine Chapel."

Rodriguez swung around at the sound of Quinn's voice, and Quinn saw the startled man's eyes focus with sudden recognition. A cruel slash of a smile crossed the sun-leathered face. With a whoop Rodriguez launched himself at Quinn in a flying leap, the blade of a long, serrated-edged knife flashing in his hands.

Sidestepping the swing, Quinn grabbed the knife hand on the follow-through and used a sweeping foot to take the man down. He landed hard but was up like a cat, slashing the knife back and forth at hip level.

Quinn ducked the hard, fast swings and blocked the last deadly lunge, flipping the croc hunter onto his back. He lay there for a minute shaking his head.

"Quinn, you son of a bitch," Rodriguez said finally. "Thought I'd never see your worthless hide again."

INSIDE Rico and Enrico's Place, over Tequila Sunrises made just right, without mixing the grenadine with the golden liquor, Quinn told

Rodriguez why he'd sought him out. He explained as little as he could, not wanting to tell Rodriguez any more than was good for him to know.

Without going into too many details, Quinn informed Rodriguez that he needed a place to hole up for a while and someone he could trust to help him make arrangements to hire a fast boat to take him to the Caymans.

"Who're you running from?"

"I'm not saying, and you don't want to find out, believe me. The less time I spend here the better. The same goes for how much you know."

"That heavy, huh?" he mused. "Sounds kinda like our old friends the spooks to me," Rodriguez surmised, sipping his drink. "Got that feel to it."

"Like I said, you don't want to know," Quinn told him. Rodriguez explained that he kept a boat out back for ocean fishing.

A shack in the Everglades, Rodriguez next explained, was what he called home. The former shadow warrior, now in the business of hunting crocodiles and alligators for sale to commercial tanneries, did a pretty good business, to hear him tell it. He agreed to put Quinn up at his place. For as long as Quinn wanted, in fact.

"HERE WE ARE," Rodriguez said, pointing to the shack built on stilts in the middle of the sea of bullrushes. "Home, sweet home."

Having originally followed narrow water channels meandering between clusters of mangrove islands, Rodriguez's airfoil boat suddenly emerged into a broad, flat region of open marshland, its limits described only by the distant horizon.

To the south, Quinn knew, lay the Atlantic Ocean and Miami, but as far as the eye could see there was nothing but swamp and sky.

Rodriguez idled the airfoil—a "Flairboot"—toward the small dock that fronted his living quarters. The Flairboot rode on a cushion of air by a process known as "flairing"—low-level, airfoil-generated flight. The craft could cruise at sustained speeds in excess of two hundred miles per hour and was not fazed in the least by any but the largest of obstacles.

Then, as Quinn made the mooring lines fast to a cleat on the dock, Rodriguez flung open the door to the shack.

While Quinn looked around at various crocodile hides, Rodriguez went to the porch out front and stoked up the barbecue in preparation for grilling the burgers and steaks he'd picked up in town.

There was ice-cold beer in the cooler, and over the brews both men soon began talking about old times. The subjects ranged from Scud-busting to behind-the-lines operations in the Hundred Hour War in Iraq that were still classified some decades later. The principals of the missions had all gone their separate ways, but the memories still remained vivid.

"How does the Frenchman fit into all this?" Rodriguez asked between mouthfuls of barbecue and beer.

"Thibodeaux is an arms dealer," Quinn replied. "He stays alive by keeping his ear to the ground and his dick in the wind. I took a chance on phoning, using a code known only to Thibodeaux, to be used only in emergencies.

"Thibodeaux gave me back the recognition code right away. He knew something was going down or he wouldn't have done so. The Frenchman's expecting me at a prearranged landing point, which I'll give the skipper of the boat as soon as we're near the beach site."

"Finding you a boat shouldn't be any major problem," Rodriguez pointed out. "I know a couple of guys who are reliable. They won't come cheap, though," he cautioned, "but they won't turn around and try to rip you off, either, not if I set up the deal, anyway."

"When can you have it taken care of?" Quinn asked, anxious to be out of the U.S. and less vulnerable to the Company's hit squads.

"Tomorrow morning," Rodriguez answered him without hesitation. "You'll know by then."

THE MEN WERE cold-eyed, deadpan, close-mouthed. Even dressed in the casual clothes that were commonplace in Cape Coral, they looked seriously out of place.

They soon made their way into Rico and Enrico's Place. The bartender stood behind the counter as before, but it was late and the house was full. One of the two men smiled thinly at the bartender. He slid Quinn's hologram toward him across the top of the bar.

"Know this guy?" he asked.

The bartender shook his head, but could not control the greed in his eyes when money crossed the moisture-filmed countertop.

"Depends who's asking," he said, smiling as another bill topped the first one.

17

It turned out that Rodriguez had some good news for Quinn.

He'd located the willing skipper of a fast boat and had already fronted the skipper a down payment from the funds provided by Quinn.

"The guy's name is Cutch," he told Quinn. "Keeps his boat not far from here. He'll be waiting for us at first light," Rodriguez went on, showing the spot marked in ink on a map of the area. "I'll take you out to him at daybreak."

Quinn checked his chronometer, noting that it was already past midnight. "We've got a couple of hours to kill yet," he said.

"No problem," Rodriguez replied, pointing to the case of beer on the floor. "I figure by the time we polish off these here hydraulic sandwiches, it'll be just the right time."

JUST BEFORE first light both men climbed aboard the Flairboot, and Rodriguez fired up the craft's powerful turbine engines. Moments later, with the big fan mounted at the stern roaring behind them, the airfoil lifted off the surface of the marsh and shot into the early dawn on a cushion of air.

Quinn glanced back at the churning white jet-wash streaming in the Flairboot's wake, which surged against the cabin's pilings. But he suddenly caught a glimpse of something else. Something that filled him with a sudden, stark dread.

Two boats, two black boats, had just appeared about three hundred yards astern.

The two black-hulled airfoil craft were now coming up fast at six o'clock, having swung into view from the mangrove island across the water from the cabin.

The stuttering flashes of automatic-weapons fire told Quinn plainly that the intentions of the men aboard the craft were anything but friendly.

Now there came a muffled thud from the pursuit craft, followed by the piercing whistle of an incoming round arrowing through the chill dawn air.

Moments later Rodriguez's cabin was blown to splinters, and a fiery blob of incandescent gases reared up into the predawn gloaming like a writhing serpent of flame.

Echoing behind them in the twilight, the menacing roar of powerful turbine engines grew louder as the pursuit craft gained on its quarry.

"Fucking spook bastards!" Rodriguez roared in anger, shaking his fist at the chase craft. "You see what they did to my house?"

"It's nothing compared to what they'll do to *us* unless we pull ahead," Quinn countered.

Rodriguez pulled the throttle out to the stops, and the Flairboot leaped to life, quickly outdistancing the pursuit craft as it left them in a cloud of spray.

But the sleek black chase boats were as fast as they came, and within seconds they were catching up again, their needle-nosed prows knifing through the Flairboot's exhaust wash, the stutters of the gimbal-mounted heavy-caliber automatic weapons pounding out a deadly staccato cadence.

"Damn, I'm hit!" Rodriguez shouted suddenly, clutching his shoulder.

"How bad?" Quinn asked, seeing blood seep between his fingers.

"I'll live," he said, already applying a pressure bandage to the wound from a first-aid kit in the boat. "Don't sweat it."

Quinn ripped the P-90 from its Velcro carrying rig, but the close-assault weapon didn't have the range or the stopping power to do much damage against the heavy-duty hardware the opposition was deploying. Rodriguez quickly solved that problem, though, by producing some exotic matériel of his own.

"Put that glorified peashooter away," he hollered at Quinn above the roar of the turbofan and the rush of the spray. "Raise the lid of the compartment in back of you. You'll find two weapons inside. They're both loaded, and there's reloads in the locker, too. Hand me the rifle—you take the heavier piece."

Quinn pulled out the two weapons. The heavier piece Rodriguez referred to was a GL100 automatic grenade rifle, outfitted with an oversize drum magazine containing twenty-five 40 mm grenade canisters with HEAT warheads.

The rifle was an LSW caseless assault weapon, its frame constructed of plastic resin. Bullpup configured, it was shorter in size than some conventional SMGs Quinn was familiar with. The LSW's stock broke open to accept a 300-round magazine, giving the weapon tremendous firepower.

"You hunt crocs with this hardware?" Quinn asked with a smile as he ported the grenade rifle and aimed its business end at the leftmost—and closest—of the two pursuit craft.

"Life's hard in the Everglades," Rodriguez replied as he charged the LSW that Quinn had handed him, chambering a live 4.73 mm caseless round. "You got every kind of scum sicko from drug runners to yacht hijackers to weird religious freaks who use these swamps as places of refuge. Believe me, Quinn, this won't be the first time I've had to use this hardware in a firefight."

Another explosion as a rifle grenade round detonated astern of the Flairboot cut short further conversation. A heartbeat later Quinn was triggering a multiround burst of the GL100, launching a salvo of 40 mm HEAT shells at the pursuing craft through gouts of salty water thrown up by the bobbing of the Flairboot.

While Quinn hammered out grenade fire at the airfoil boats on their tail, Rodriguez was firing the much lighter LSW one-handed and over-the-shoulder fashion while keeping a firm grip on the Flairboot's steering wheel.

Quinn kept laying down saturation fire from the GL100, launching multiple bursts of high-explosive shells in pulsed salvos to generate a continuous wave front that produced no kills but seemed largely responsible for keeping the chase craft at bay.

After successive tries Quinn got his target taped. A 5-round salvo of HEAT shells caught the pursuit craft on the left head-on, slamming into its prow with devastating consequences for the boat and its crew.

Thundering in the dawn, the violent explosion lifted the craft's stern above the weed-choked surface of the great salt marsh on a cataract of blinding yellow flame.

Traveling at high speed, the airfoil boat went out of control. Canting over into a barrel roll and trailing spirals of thick black smoke, it went careening on its side across the swamp surface like a huge, flat stone sent skipping across a pond, skipping once, twice, and then smashing into a small mangrove island and exploding.

Borne skyward on a pillar of flame, the huge ball of incandescent gases rose into the air. From out of the fireball, pieces of the blazing wreckage went pinwheeling into the still-dark pre-dawn sky.

"Nice shooting, Quinn," Rodriguez said, "but the other one's still on us."

"And likely to be a lot more careful now," Quinn added as he reloaded a fresh 25-round grenade magazine into the weapon's receiver and locked in the magazine, "considering what happened to the point craft."

A cluster of small mangrove islands was coming up fast off the Flairboot's port bow. Rodriguez headed for the island group, telling Quinn that he'd probably be able to shake the pursuit craft in the maze of twisting channels that meandered through it.

Rodriguez whipped the fast and highly maneuverable craft into the first channel he was able to reach. Quinn could see the lone pursuit craft follow right behind them, determinedly staying in their jet-wash.

He launched another salvo of GL100 grenade fire as Rodriguez zigzagged between the islands at high speed, and they came back out into open swamp several minutes later with the pursuit craft nowhere to be seen.

"Looks like maybe I shook them," Rodriguez commented as he opened the throttles full again and pointed the Flairboot's sleek prow toward the rendezvous point with the fast boat.

"You spoke too soon," Quinn corrected him scant minutes later. Off to starboard the chase boat was now barreling right at them as it popped up from the concealment of the farthermost mangrove island, pointing its prow toward them while .50-caliber automatic fire blazed from its port and starboard guns. "They probably just ran circles around the islands, figuring they'd pick us up sooner or later."

The pace of pursuit quickly gathered momentum again. Quinn and Rodriguez traded fire with the crew of the pursuing craft, but the pursuers were less reckless now and cautiously maintained their distance. The .50-caliber guns they carried gave them a range advantage on their quarry, and the kill crew could afford to maintain a comfortable distance, exploiting the superiority of their industrial-strength firepower.

"Did I see a jerrican back there?" Quinn asked Rodriguez after considering ways to break the stalemate.

"Sure," he returned. "Carry one in case I run out of gas. So what?"

Quinn didn't answer, now crunching the numbers for survival. He already had the plastic container in his hands and was checking the can to make certain it was full.

The powerful vortex of wind produced by the big fan mounted at the rear of the Flairboot had given him an idea, the notion of a desperate gambit he could try to turn the tables on the covert terminators hell-bent on wiping them out.

Quinn found an inlet through which he could pour the gasoline, dumping the entire container into the wide-mouthed duct that was normally intended for engine lubricants.

The Flairboot's powerful turbofans took care of the rest, dispersing the liquid in the form of a fine mist that fanned out in the wake of the Flairboot in a rapidly spreading cone of aerosolized high octane fuel.

When the Flairboot had outdistanced the cloud of aerosolized gasoline, Quinn raised the GL100 and aimed the grenade launcher at the center of the cloud, which he could see as a faintly sparkling brownish haze caused by the dispersion of the slanting rays of the rising sun through the low-hanging curtain of mist.

The pursuing craft was just at that moment speeding directly into the floating cloud of gasoline vapor. The airfoil's skipper must have flashed on what was about to happen, because as Quinn fired a multiround burst of grenade shells at it, he saw the pursuit craft suddenly swerve hard to port, its jet-wash turning white in an elongated S shape.

The game was up for the pursuit craft, though, and both Quinn and its passengers knew it. The proximity-fuzed grenade detonated before the chase craft could put sufficient distance between itself and the aerosolized cloud of highly volatile marine fuel.

The detonating grenade canisters set off the inflammable mixture of air and gasoline. In essence it produced a ferocious blast effect—the direct equivalent of the detonation of a fuel-air explosive.

In a swift chain reaction the pursuing craft became engulfed in a massive firestorm as the aerosolized droplets of gasoline ignited, producing a concussive blast of devastating force.

Quinn saw the boat, which was now enveloped in a churning vortex of flame, break up instantly, then disintegrate completely as its own fuel tanks caught fire and explosives on-board cooked off in the tremendous heat.

The wreckage of the pursuit craft sailed high into the air to fall back onto the placid waters of the swamp minutes later, hissing with steam. Fragments of the boat lay everywhere, burning amid the cattails and bullrushes of the great salt marsh.

"See you in hell!" Rodriguez shouted behind him as he whipped the Flairboot back onto its original course toward the fast boat that would soon take Quinn out of Florida.

18

"There she is," Rodriguez said, pointing across the Flairboot's starboard bow.

Quinn saw the cruiser silhouetted against the slowly lightening horizon. The boat was a sleek black craft, with the telltale rounded contours of a low-observable stealth configuration. Quinn felt grateful to his friend. Rodriguez had chosen well.

The croc hunter pulled the Flairboot up to the port bow of the cruiser as Quinn saw a figure in cutoff shorts and a white T-shirt emerge from the cabin and stand on the deck. He was carrying a boat hook. As Rodriguez nudged the Flairboot close to the cruiser's hull, her skipper helped them make fast to the stern and hailed them aboard.

"What do we do with you?" Quinn asked Rodriguez, whose shoulder wound sustained near the start of the chase was now throbbing painfully.

"Well," Rodriguez ventured, "my house is burned to the waterline, there's an army of kill-

ers fixing to nail my stones to the outhouse wall
and my arm's all shot up. Guess I don't have
much to lose by tagging along."

They went below, and the skipper got out a
first-aid kit. He looked over Rodriguez's wound
and pronounced that it would be all right as soon
as they dug the slug fragments out of his arm.

"This here's Cutch," Rodriguez told Quinn.
"Forgot to introduce you to the skipper of this
scow. As you can see, she is one of the meanest-
looking boats in these waters."

"Glad to know you," Cutch said, extending
his hand for Quinn to shake. "But don't call *La
Negra* a 'scow,'" he went on only half-jokingly
as he laid out surgical instruments from his first-
aid kit. "I'm proud of her. She's state-of-the-art
from her long-range radar to her hard-chine dis-
placement hull. I'll show you the wheelhouse
when I'm through with Rodriguez. You look like
a guy who appreciates class."

Quinn did indeed appreciate what he saw. *La
Negra*'s wheelhouse was stuffed to the nines with
ECMs—sophisticated electronic countermea-
sures equipment—featuring advanced radars and
jamming gear. The low-slung, stealthy ship had
obviously been designed and built with the eva-

sion of pursuit and interdiction a prime consideration.

Quinn didn't ask why Cutch had outfitted his boat in this particular fashion, but he didn't really have to. He could guess at the various types of missions that a runner like Cutch would be well paid for with a craft such as *La Negra* at his disposal.

As for Cutch himself, he looked like basically a stand-up dude, but Quinn picked up signals telling him to be careful of what he said and did around *La Negra*'s skipper. One tip-off was Cutch's smile; the smile said one thing—Don't worry about me, I'm on your side. But the eyes—bright on the outside, cold on the inside—said another.

Cutch throttled up, and soon the sleek craft was beating the dawn into the open ocean. Not too long after first light they were miles from the coast of the Florida panhandle, tooling along at a brisk thirty-five-knot pace thanks to *La Negra*'s powerful twin fuel-injected engines.

It was early afternoon when Cutch came back to the stern and told his two passengers that there was some trouble on the horizon.

"Picking up a bogie," he explained, pointing to one of the many rack-mounted VDTs on the bridge console. "Looks like a Coast Guard cutter from its radar echo. Yep, that's exactly what it is. Shit. They've locked on to us!"

Quinn watched the progress of the ship icon moving across the center of the computer-enhanced radar screen. Cutch continued to scan the banks of equipment, taking his eyes off his VDTs only long enough to punch in sequences of commands at the console keyboards.

"Yeah, they're definitely after us," Cutch said, "but not to worry," he continued as he flipped some switches and punched a series of lighted buttons. Pretty soon the blip began to fade away as the equipment flashed constantly updated status reports on its array of multiple screens. "I invested a lot of bread on ECM equipment. The electronic jamming these little beauties can deliver has kept more than one bogie off my tail. Looks like they just did it again."

By evening Quinn and Rodriguez were back in the wheelhouse. Cutch informed his two passengers that they were only about forty-five minutes away from making landfall at Grand Cayman.

"I think it's about time you gave me the landing coordinates," he said to Quinn.

"You're right," Quinn replied, asking Cutch to show him a nautical map and sketching the coordinates as he laid the map across a chart table. "Here they are."

"Great," Cutch replied with a nod as he studied the map. "I know the landing zone well." Suddenly there was a compact black H&K submachine gun bulging in his fist. "Now I'd appreciate it if both you and my good buddy Rodriguez here drop down on the deck with your hands clasped behind your pointy little heads."

"Cutch, you miserable ratprick," Rodriguez hollered. "What the hell kind of double cross is this?"

Cutch laughed.

"The *only* kind, my reptile-skinning friend," he replied. "You pay me to get you someplace. They—that omnipotent 'they' who I never ask questions about—pay me even more for turning you in to them. Twice the bread. That's the kind of double cross I'm into—the kind that *pays*."

Cutch jerked the SMG downward and repeated his command for his two captives to lie on the deck. He was getting impatient now, and his trigger finger was developing a distinct itch.

"Surprise, surprise," Rodriguez told Cutch, now smiling himself. "I spiked your gun, shit-head."

To Quinn, he said, "I didn't want to tell you, good buddy, but I didn't completely trust our fearless leader, Cutch. He had the fastest boat in the state and happened to be available on short notice. But trust him, that I didn't."

To Cutch, he continued, "Your popgun ain't worth squat. Now hand it over."

"Don't try to bullshit me," Cutch snarled. "You didn't even know where it was. Now get on the floor."

Rodriguez took a step toward Cutch, who brandished the gun and told him not to make another move or he'd fire. Rodriguez immediately took another step forward. Cutch pulled the SMG's trigger.

Cutch's face came apart in a crimson spray as the rear of the SMG exploded at him. Flung backward by the sudden blast, he did a quarter-turn and came to rest in a semicrouch with his mutilated head leaving a bloody track as it slid down an equipment console.

"Poor dumb asshole," Rodriguez said as he dragged Cutch's body from the wheelhouse. "I always wondered why he didn't end up shark food sooner." Quinn watched Rodriguez drag Cutch over to the gunwale and throw him over the side of the boat.

This close in to shore, sharks were guaranteed to be within minutes of the floating body. In fact, it only took seconds for the first dorsal fin to appear. In a matter of seconds it was followed by others.

"That's a mako," Rodriguez said, looking over the railing at the stern of *La Negra.* "There's two tigers, and that one's a gray. Our friend Cutch won't be around much longer to pollute the ocean."

Moments later, true to his prediction, Cutch's floating body was pulled below the waterline by voracious jaws and torn to pieces by the insatiable predators of the deep.

Quinn went into the wheelhouse and turned his attention to the bank of instruments for a few minutes. Apart from *La Negra*'s advanced ECM and navigational devices, operating the bridge equipment would pose no problem. He would be able to pilot the craft into the landing zone without any trouble, Quinn was certain.

Twenty minutes later the sleek black craft slid toward the deserted beach zone. Quinn used high-powered binoculars to zoom in on the figures that had appeared on the sands and were waving at them.

Anchoring *La Negra* in the shallows, Quinn and Rodriguez waded ashore and followed the two local islanders up onto the beach. On the rise above the beach zone a black stretch limo was parked.

The rear door of the limo swung open as Quinn and Rodriguez approached, and Quinn caught sight of the Frenchman's face inside the big car's air-conditioned interior.

MISSION LOG TWO:

Vortex

19

Griffin brought the motorbike to a halt and killed the ignition. The steep-sided gully, scoured out by thousands of years of flash flooding, was well screened from view of the road above it. To further conceal the bike he covered it with a tarp and piled dry scrub over the entire affair.

The South Dakota night was moonless and pitch-black, but to Griffin, equipped with an IR-sensing internal video display, it looked as if the terrain were illuminated by the light of an intense emerald sun, the road clearly visible against the shimmering green electronic viewfield.

He began running at a trot, quickly gathering speed until he was surging forward at sixty miles per hour. At that rate he would reach his destination in only scant minutes.

Griffin's estimate was right on the money. The twenty-foot-high galvanized chain-link perimeter fence encircled an installation comprised of low-rise blockhouses and inflatable Quonset huts.

Standing still, Griffin scanned the apron of bare earth surrounding the perimeter fence.

A series of glowing white dashes overlaid the light-amplified image of the insertion zone. The IVD flashed azimuth coordinates, showing Griffin that the fence was ringed inside and out by a sophisticated field-effect intruder-detection system.

Any break in the magnetic field generated by nodes buried in the apron of earth would trigger an alarm.

The IVD next showed Griffin a full-motion diagram of a human body leaping over the fence and landing precisely ten feet within the installation compound: the way inside was clear.

Griffin terminated his scan and began running toward the fence. He gained speed quickly and, just beyond the rim of buried motion sensors, he jumped.

Griffin's running leap catapulted him over the top of the perimeter fence, and he dropped to the ground, the pneumatic shock absorbers in his cybernetically enhanced legs cushioning the impact of the fall.

Inside the base security station some distance away, an intruder alarm sounded. Although Griffin had landed clear of the buried sensor nodes, the vibrations of his feet touching down had been picked up by other hidden sensors.

The alarm had only lasted a second, though, and the duty officer scanned the base perimeter through the banks of low-light television cameras that ringed the installation.

He saw nothing to indicate that the alarm had been caused by anything other than mechanical error. Yet someone or something might have triggered the perimeter alarm. He logged an electronic mail note for technicians to check the perimeter security system and returned to watching television.

Just then there was the sound of splintering glass, and the guard looked up to see a black-clad muscular man punch bare-knuckle through the bulletproof window, then leap into the control room through the shattered frame.

Badly scared but still in control, the guard drew his automatic and fired at the intruder. Regular shooting on the base firing range had paid off. Reacting quickly, he'd succeeded in putting two rounds squarely into the intruder's heart region.

The intruder kept coming, though. He took the gun away from the dumbfounded man before he could fire another shot, then turned it around and stuck its muzzle into the guard's right eye. He squeezed off two bullets in lightning succession, which blew pieces of the guard's cornea and brain out through the rear of his skull and dropped him instantly to the floor.

Sparks cascaded and jets of flaming ozone shot from the multiple-monitor banks as Griffin pile-drived his fist into each of them, rendering the perimeter cameras inoperable.

As he moved quickly through the acrid smoke that was now filling the guard booth, the flashing IVD display showed him the location of the specific warehouse he sought.

Sprinting away from the trashed security station, Griffin crossed the open compound toward one of the long blockhouse structures to his right. The particular blockhouse he was interested in was a dump for highly exotic armament, armament of the kind Griffin was much in need of.

He reached the target area just as the guard who was walking his post turned a corner and came abreast of the shadowed section of wall at which Griffin had flattened.

Now behind the sentinel, Griffin reached out, grasping the soldier's neck with his right hand.

The sentry tore at the hand holding his throat, making gargling noises and kicking out his legs as Griffin hoisted him three feet off the ground, quickly strangling him.

When the sentry went jellyfish limp, Griffin shoved his flaccid body into the concealment of a big trash bin where it would not be discovered until he was long gone from the installation. He broke legs and arms to make sure the corpse would fit inside.

The iron door that gave access to the warehouse was locked, but Griffin punched through its center, reached inside and unlatched it from within.

In seconds he had bent the petaled surface back into shape, pulled the door back in its frame and was inside the storage depot.

Overhead floodlights lit the warehouse area in which palleted weapons were stacked throughout the expanse of the enormous dump. The glowing white dashes overlaid on the scene by his IVD showed Griffin the exact location of the arms cache he was intent on ransacking.

When Griffin reached it, he saw that his destination was a locked vault door made out of stainless steel that he reckoned must be several feet thick.

He placed his ear to the huge door of the vault and touched his fingers to the dial. He listened carefully as he turned the dial this way and that, able to hear the tumblers click into place.

A smile crossed his lips as he pulled the safe door back on its hinges and entered the vault. Like the exterior of the storage warehouse, it was glaringly lit by bright overhead floods.

Housed along its gleaming steel walls were what Griffin had come for.

The squat black canisters, stored in special shockproof frames on shelves against the walls, didn't appear to be especially dangerous. But that was because they had not been designed to draw attention. They had been designed to destroy, and that they did exceptionally well.

They were nuclear explosives, known in military jargon as SADMs—special atomic demolition munitions.

The SADMs were extremely small but extremely lethal. Griffin would need two of the micronukes to accomplish his purposes.

He took these and slid them into a special carrying pouch that was slung on his back.

Having gotten what he came for, Griffin then turned and swiftly exited the vault, locking its stainless-steel door behind him and then resetting the tumblers to their original positions with a few deft movements of his fingers.

Moving quickly from the warehouse, Griffin sprinted across the base compound, exfiltration now his goal.

At roughly the same time, the dead duty officer's relief walked up to the security station and blinked twice, not able to believe the carnage he saw in front of him.

The duty officer might not have believed his eyes, but his state of panic and confusion didn't last very long.

Acting quickly, he grabbed the commo unit from his belt and began transmitting an emergency code that would automatically throw the entire base into action as soon as computers linked to the commo net received it.

Griffin was soon confronted by a detachment of soldiers armed with M-20 caseless assault weapons. When he didn't halt as he was ordered to do, they opened fire, sighting on Griffin at point-blank range.

Scores of bullets slammed into Griffin's body, but he continued moving ahead despite the punishing fusillade of high-velocity rounds striking him in a massed fire front.

Pulling grenades from chest webbing, the cyborg flipped the compact black balls at the troops, targeting the high-energy submunitions with computerized eye-hand coordination to explode in a series of phased airbursts.

The blast waves from the precisely thrown grenades went off with devastating effect, blowing off limbs in a maelstrom of spinning steel splinters. Kicking the dead and the dying out of his way, Griffin moved toward the exfiltration point shown him by his IVD.

He continued toward the gate as Humvees now roared off in pursuit, the MAG heavy machineguns mounted atop the vehicles already firing 7.62 mm rounds at the running figure who zigzagged with such speed that the soldiers couldn't track him.

The troops commanding the pursuit vehicles could not believe their eyes when Griffin leaped over the twenty-foot-high security fence and sprinted off into the predawn darkness at breakneck pace.

The personnel carriers shrieked from the main gate, pursuing the fleeing man.

They did not get far.

Griffin reached into his pocket and produced a remote detonation device. Pressing one, then another, of the series of buttons studding the punchpad, he triggered the concealed charges he'd slotted along the road surface.

The Humvees were caught in the whirlwind of blast effect and summarily burst into flame.

Within seconds the fleeing man had jumped onto his cycle and tore away from the hide site in the gully at better than one hundred miles per hour.

Minutes later he swung the bike onto a turn-off where an eighteen-wheeler truck was parked.

Its rear hatch was open, and a wide metal ramp sloped onto the surface of the road. Griffin roared the bike up the ramp and lurched to a screaming stop just behind the cab of the truck.

Pulling up the ramp after him and closing the rear hatch, Griffin hustled into the cab and barreled the truck onto the highway.

20

Air Force One was a Boeing aerospace plane capable of suborbital flight at multi-Mach speeds. Its amenities included communications equipment hardened against jamming and distortion by nuclear blast and EMP, spacious sleeping and dining quarters, a dispensary equipped with a fully functional operating room and a conference chamber that was the equal of anything in the subbasement strategy-planning center situated beneath the White House.

In fact, the President preferred conducting affairs of state at ninety thousand feet. He was fast earning a reputation as spending more time in the air than on the ground as he shuttled from capital to capital in pursuit of his political agenda.

He had come to find the psychological edge of knowing that, although he enjoyed the mobility of reaching any point on the globe in under two hours, his tie lines to NORAD, SAC, the CIA, NSA and the host of other federal agencies vital to the implementation of policy were as secure as if he were sitting in the Oval Office. And Air Force One provided another advantage over the Oval Office: he could get away from the first lady for indefinite periods of time.

All this to the contrary, the President now felt more perplexed than he had been throughout all the crises he had faced since his inauguration, as he sat at the head of the horseshoe-shaped conference table. Surrounding him were Sylvain Covington, Director of Central Intelligence, Secretary of Defense Robert Castagna, and Brigadier General Mitchell Freeth, Head of DARPA. Also present was Neil Simmons, the President's communications director.

Freeth had the floor. Bringing the President up to date on the beginnings of the crisis, he stood in front of the one-hundred-by-fifty-inch convex digital screen that flashed a montage of images. There were unclothed male bodies lying in transparent cocoons. The bodies were unmoving. The cocoons were linked to flashing banks of computers by long rubber umbilicals.

"This was the beginning of Upcard," Freeth said, the thin red beam of his laser pointer touching parts of the screen. "For decades America's top fighting men, members of elite Special Forces units like Delta, did not suspect that during routine physicals they were donating tissue that was being used in an ongoing experiment in cloning what, for want of a better term, we'll call the 'super commando.' ''

The holographic scenes shifted to a group of camo-fatigued troops undergoing rigorous physical training, hand-to-hand combat and weapons instruction.

"In the midnineties," Freeth continued, "a top secret military venture—Project Upcard—finally succeeded in producing an advanced biological weapon intended for combat use—a supersolider clone. Upcard reached the technological break-even point in the late nineties, when cloned newborns were produced. These were then subjected to shock-rearing techniques designed to render them insensitive to pain and suffering and fed special diets laced with molecular-engineered steroidal substances to produce extreme muscular development while at the same time increasing their brainpower by many orders of magnitude.

"Intensive commando training completed the development of each clone, enabling them to function in a variety of battlefield environments. The clones were intended to be the forerunners of special commando squads capable of being deployed into radioactive, biological or chemical battlefields, where normal humans could not function as ground assets."

The DARPA director paused, and the holographic montage shifted to scenes depicting live-fire training exercises where the supersoldier clones moved across battlezones unaffected by clouds of poison gas and high levels of radiation.

"A handful of fully functional clones survived to maturity in the rigorous Upcard trials. However, all developed serious psychological aberrations that made them highly dangerous. During the final phase of testing the clones went berserk and wiped out almost all personnel at an ultrasecret DARPA research facility where they were being put through their final paces. The story was suppressed in the media, but the up-shot was that the clones were ordered euthanized in the interests of national security.

"My colleagues in the CIA," Freeth went on with a glance at Covington, "thought otherwise. They had funded the project and instead of destroying the fruits of this multibillion-dollar military research undertaking—especially when knowing that other world powers were working along the same lines—succeeded in saving the most advanced of the clones. One in particular, was singled out for special treatment.

"In a specially constructed chamber deep within the earth, this last and most highly developed clone was connected to a virtual reality interface. In this deep and artificially induced autistic state, augmented with psychoactive drugs, the clone was fed cybernetic input that made it believe it was engaged in perpetual combat. The clone, code-named Griffin, was to have been kept indefinitely in this state," Freeth concluded, "but of course recent events have demonstrated the folly of such a plan. My colleague from Central Intelligence will take over now, Mr. President," Freeth said as he returned to his seat, handing the pointer to Covington, who rose to take his place beside the holo display.

Covington keystroked in a command set at the keypad on the conference table, and the on-screen images shifted to contemporary scenes of mass destruction. The first of these scenes showed the empty cyberpod chamber from which Griffin had been released.

"Mr. President, we don't have the big picture yet, but we do know some things. We know that Griffin was released by this man—" the scene abruptly shifted to a still shot of a man of medium build in a lab technician's coat "—one Dexter Barasheens, a cybernetic systems specialist under Agency contract. Some forty-eight hours after Griffin's release, Barasheens ostensibly committed suicide in his Las Vegas hotel room.

"But we believe that he was actually murdered, silenced to prevent him from revealing his ultimate link to this man—" again the scene shifted, showing a heavyset, goateed man with piercing green eyes "—one Sergei Korniyenko, a ranking KGB official who also shot himself less than one week after Barasheens's death. In Korniyenko's case we understand that he genuinely took his own life. We have no facts, only theories, but we believe that it was Korniyenko who sanctioned the release of Griffin."

"Why?" interjected the President.

"That we don't know as yet, sir," Covington went on. "However, we suspect that the release was attempted as a plan to discredit ARGUS by linking this technological feat in world opinion with the image of a rampaging clone, leading to an outcry to dismantle the system."

Covington shifted the video display through scenes of Griffin's assaults on the Iron Mountain storage facility and the high-security weapons dump in South Dakota, scenes depicting the awesome power of the single clone pitted against squads of armed men and mechanized units.

"We suspect strongly, sir, that the initial rationale used for releasing Griffin can no longer explain his actions. Korniyenko's suicide argues that he found himself in a position where he was no longer in control and was forced to take his own life. Griffin's actions are not consonant with the disinformation scenario we have put forth. In short, we are convinced at this point that Griffin is pursuing an agenda of his own with a desired outcome known only to himself."

The President stared at the procession of high-resolution images of Griffin. "Freeze it right there, will you, Sly?" he asked Covington, who promptly complied. The President put his hand to his chin. "You've left out two important points, as far as I can see," he told Covington.

"What would those be, sir?" the DCI asked.

"Firstly," the President said, "I'm still unclear on what precisely Griffin has taken from those installations and why he's taken them. You say the first installation was a data-storage facility, and the second was what—an arms depot?"

"Correct, sir," Covington replied. "As to the nature of the items removed, we do not as yet know what—if anything at all—was removed by Griffin from Iron Mountain. And while we know that two subkiloton nuclear devices were removed from the South Dakota facility, we cannot discern their use in support of any grand scheme. The nukes are far too low-yield and far too clean to warrant the trouble he went to in order to obtain them. A quantity of high-energy explosive, much easier to obtain on the international arms market, would have proven far more destructive."

"I see," the President said, now leaning forward and slapping his palm on the table. "As for my second question, you'd damn well better have a good explanation. Why does that clone look identical to the action operative code-named Nomad? Why in the name of hell does it look like *Quinn?*" the President demanded. "I want no equivocation, no evasions. You shoot straight on this one, Sly."

Covington looked at the brigadier general and the secretary of defense, who both averted their eyes before he turned back to the President. "Sir," he began, clearing his throat, "you recall that my colleague from DARPA told you earlier in this presentation that the Upcard subjects were cloned from experimental Special Forces subjects, without the knowledge or consent of the donors?''

"I heard,'' the President said impatiently. "Get on with it!''

"Sir, the final clone, the one that showed the greatest, um, skill and promise—that clone was produced from tissue explanted from Quinn,'' Covington concluded.

The President was silent for a long minute.

"Thank you, Sly,'' he said in a low voice. "You can sit down now. As for my reaction to all this, gentlemen, needless to say, I want Griffin stopped, no matter how or what it takes. But I want to state this categorically—none of you are unaware of the personal sacrifice which Quinn has recently rendered not only the United States of America but the entire community of mankind in neutralizing the Prometheus threat.

"If not for his selfless valor, I do not doubt that our world would be a very different and very much less free place than it is today. Listen to me and listen to me well—I want Quinn fully briefed on the crisis and I furthermore want him to act as the spear point of the operation.''

The President rose to leave.

"But, sir,'' Freeth and Covington called out simultaneously.

But the President was already out of the briefing room and on his way to his personal quarters.

He had a great deal of reflecting to do. There was a lot at stake, including the personal fate of an unsung American patriot: the man code-named Nomad.

21

Three paramilitary assets comprised the strike unit designated Cobra Blue. The team had infiltrated the operation zone the previous day, arriving in two waves on separate commercial flights originating from Logan in Boston and JFK in New York, a strategy designed to attract a bare minimum of undesired attention.

Assets designated Trident and Emerald posed as a tourist couple carrying American passports and flying coach. The third strike team member, designated Skate, arrived on Grand Cayman Island later that same day, traveling as a corporate executive and occupying a seat in the first-class compartment at the front of the aircraft.

Support infrastructure already in place in Grand Cayman had secured the *Sonrisas,* a cabin cruiser berthed at a local marina, to be deployed as a launch platform for the covert paramilitary hard probe and subsequent termination effort.

Skate found Trident and Emerald awaiting him on board the *Sonrisas* upon his arrival early that afternoon. It was a clear, bright day, with temperatures and humidity both comfortably low, and the trio promptly set out on what would appear to outside observers to be no more than a pleasure cruise in the island vicinity.

However, the *Sonrisas* was no mere pleasure craft, just as its casually attired occupants were not what they appeared, either. The cruiser was stocked with weapons and equipped with sophisticated surveillance gear, and the telemetry received from orbiting spy satellites was instantly made available for the strike team's review.

Skate, whose assignment was to precision engineer the action from initial probe to ultimate strike immediately went below and got to work, poring over the maps, position and situation reports and other data received from orbiting surveillance platforms as Trident piloted the *Sonrisas* out beyond the barrier reef with its placid lagoon and into the Caribbean.

After checking the weapons stores already on board the cruiser upon their arrival and assuring themselves that all was in readiness, Trident and Emerald took advantage of the brief slack time to engage in fishing and snorkeling in the crystal blue waters of the Caribbean.

Their activities provided the added cover of offering convincing evidence to any observers that those on board the *Sonrisas* were no more than they appeared to be: American tourists enjoying a Caribbean holiday, the perennial innocents abroad.

By early evening Skate, who had been in the cabin belowdecks poring over satellite-generated maps of the area and intelligence briefs received by secure telefax, had devised what he deemed a workable plan of assault on the team's assigned target.

Calling Trident and Emerald into the electronically sterile cabin where he had worked alone until then, Skate reviewed the plan he had established and, after weighing their suggestions and feedback, polished and finalized the team's blueprint for destruction.

It was decided that the strike would be executed at 2330 hours, and none of the trio had any doubts that it would succeed.

WITH THE COOLNESS of evening, the scent of jacaranda growing wild on the villa's grounds infused the tropical air with its cloyingly sweet scent.

To the west, over the ocean, storm clouds backlit by the setting sun glowed a luminous magenta.

Quinn had gone out to the villa's poolside area with the intention of taking the time for a much-needed workout while some daylight still remained.

The Frenchman's opulent estate was a gilded cage, and Quinn had grown bored and edgy while awaiting Thibodeaux's emissary to deliver his ultimatum to the CIA bureau chief in the Caymans.

His message to the Company warned them that he was prepared to go to both the media and congressional Intelligence oversight groups with what he knew about Upcard. Quinn wanted his name cleared and the hunt for him called off. He would not willingly be crucified in the name of national security.

Quinn knew that the pace of business in these islands was painfully slow and because of the Junkaloo—the Caymans' equivalent of Mardi Gras in the States—the delay would be all the greater.

Nevertheless, he was feeling increasingly like a penned-in panther and needed to iron out the kinks on a purely physical level.

Quinn began a sequence of hwa-rang-do offensive and defensive movements, starting from a completely stationary position to quickly launch into a complicated yet unified sequence of lightning-fast blocks, kicks, hand blows and finger strikes.

As he progressed through the martial arts *kata,* his concentration became more and more acutely focused on the imaginary combat that he waged in his mind.

He became completely absorbed in the flow and progression of the martial arts *kata* as what some master fighters called ''it'' took over and Quinn's consciousness was merged with the sinuous movements of his body.

Lashing out, blocking with hands and feet, thrusting from side to side and snapping off deadly combinations of front, side and back kicks, Quinn was swept up in a storm of action that carried him with it until his energies were spent.

After completing his workout, Quinn plunged into the pool and swam a few laps, emerging from the water with a little of the edge taken off his restlessness.

As he sat by a poolside table, Thibodeaux and Rodriguez came toward him from out of the

main house. Rodriguez was dressed outlandishly as a pirate of the Spanish main, complete
with tricornered hat, eye patch and flintlock pistol jammed in his belt beside his ever-present
knife.

"Your message has been delivered," the
Frenchman told Quinn. "You must excuse our
delay, however, as our friend Rodriguez here insisted on stopping by a local costume shop after
he consented to accompany me to the Junkaloo
tonight."

"Funny," Quinn said, but he barely smiled as
Rodriguez pointed the flintlock at Quinn, pulled
the trigger and a sign reading Bang! shot out of
the muzzle of the old-fashioned gun. "As for my
reply, what kind of wait are we talking, Thibodeaux?"

"Ah, that is another matter entirely, sir," the
portly Frenchman responded with a laugh.
"With the pageant on, it could take days until we
know of anything definite. However, as you
yourself are doubtless well aware, as long as you
are a guest in my humble home, you are protected against the possibility of becoming the
victim of foul play. Not even your cowboy
government would risk the embarrassment of
mounting a strike here."

"I hope you're right," Quinn said to Thibodeaux.

"Then I trust that your hope is not built upon a false foundation," the Frenchman responded with a laugh as he puffed on his cigar. "As for waiting, I would suggest that you accompany us to tonight's festivities. There are a number of nubile young ladies of my acquaintance to whom I could introduce you in the event that you desire companionship. Rodriguez is, I need not even add, extremely anxious to meet them."

"I'm sure he is," Quinn told the Frenchman, "but I'll pass just the same."

"So be it, then," Thibodeaux told Quinn. "There are still a few hours left before we decamp for the town center in the event that you should change your mind. If you don't, though, then my advice to you, my friend, is don't wait up. Rodriguez and I will probably be quite late tonight."

With that the Frenchman and Rodriguez turned and went back into the house. After they had gone, Quinn plunged into the pool and swam another few laps while heat lightning flickered on the brilliantly lit horizon.

COBRA BLUE DEPLOYED onto the villa estate, climbing over the stone-and-concrete security wall and skirting the perimeter alarm devices installed by Thibodeaux, their nature and precise location revealed to Skate by his Intel and taken into account while detailing the operation on board the *Sonrisas*.

The team wore black battle dress of a Kevlar weave over bright tropical leisure clothes and were outfitted with compact SITES Spectre SMGs.

Skate's weapon was a Chinese-made Mauser machine pistol, the merc's personal favorite, augmented with a laser designator scope.

They would shed the blacksuits on extraction from the strike zone, drive to the marina and pilot the *Sonrisas* to a pickup point out at sea, where an amphibious plane would be waiting.

Quickly reaching the delivery entrance of the manor house located at the rear of the kitchen, Skate neutralized the electronic lock on its door using a credit-card-sized jammer, and the trio commenced their probe, SMGs ported at the hip for lightning deployment.

No resistance was encountered within, and Cobra Blue moved on through the villa, alert for the presence of their designated target, the man who had been marked for swift, silent termination.

The villa appeared deserted, devoid even of the presence of domestic staff members, and the strike trio climbed the stairs leading to the bedroom area after ascertaining that the lower level of the house was in fact empty.

Probing silently, they progressed toward the master bedroom. Upon reaching it, they saw that the lights were turned on beyond the door, which, though closed, was not locked.

Emerald and Trident waited on either side of the door frame with full-auto weapons poised for "room cleaning." Skate pushed against the door, entering the room on a half roll with the Mauser machine pistol already tracking left and right while Emerald and Trident simultaneously entered the bedroom behind him, their weapons poised for striking.

They found that the room was empty. The probing beams of the laser target designator mounted atop Skate's Mauser augered into the empty bed, across the unoccupied bathroom opening away from it and skittered along the blank walls of the untenanted bedchamber.

With professional skill the strike detail searched the bathroom and the veranda beyond the high French doors and established beyond a doubt that their target was nowhere in the immediate vicinity. Emerald and Trident turned to Skate, who shrugged his broad shoulders.

The target was supposed to have been found here tonight.

Perhaps he still would be.

Skate gestured, using prearranged hand signals to indicate that the team was to search the house again as he deactivated the laser designator.

Continuing to probe silently through the upper story of the villa, the strike team came to the guest wing some minutes later.

There they found another room with its lights turned on. Skate heard the sound of running water coming from the bathroom in a small hallway beyond the main room onto which the door opened.

The trio burst into the room just as Quinn was emerging from the shower, toweling his hair dry. He stopped short as the long lance of coherent ruby light from Skate's target-designating laser touched the center of his chest.

Skate smiled.

The mission might not have to be a scrub after all, he thought. The execution squad had at least found someone on the premises.

Perhaps he could lead them to their target. Perhaps he could lead them to the Frenchman. Perhaps they would take out their man tonight after all.

22

With a gun muzzle jammed into the small of his back, Quinn threaded his way through the jubilant crowds thronging Georgetown's main street.

By now the Junkaloo was already in full swing, and the celebrants were pumped up with the party spirit, supplemented by liberal applications of the potent local dark rum. Gaudy parade floats wended their way slowly along the crowded avenue while outlandishly attired revelers seethed and milled about like shoals of bizarre tropical fish.

The irony that Quinn had found himself drawn into the center of a hit attempt against his benefactor was not lost on somebody who himself was the subject of a massive clandestine hunt as Skate prodded him forward, Emerald and Trident flanking Quinn and keeping lookout.

Quinn wondered how the merc trio would react if they knew that their captive was a target far more valuable to them than Thibodeaux could ever be. He was damn glad they didn't, though.

The Frenchman might be faithful to his word about Company assets not treading on his turf, thought Quinn to himself.

But this dictum apparently did not go as far as Thibodeaux's own business interests were concerned. From what Quinn had been able to glean from the discussion of the trio, they had been sent by one of the Frenchman's business rivals to settle an old score once and for all.

The trio conversed in French regarding their plans. However, it was a patois or dialect—likely Corsican—that Quinn only partially understood, especially since they laced their speech with code words known only to themselves and unintelligible to him.

Still, Quinn didn't need an interpreter to fully comprehend the basic parameters of the strike team's mission.

Knowing that their objective was to scratch the Frenchman, Quinn could easily extrapolate that they planned to use him as a Judas goat, a means of getting close to Thibodeaux and at that point opening up on their target.

In the confusion of the Junkaloo, escape would not be a difficult matter for the trio of contract killers.

In fact, the tactical blunder that they had committed by staging their execution strike concurrently with the festival would turn out to work to their advantage in the long run by effectively covering their getaway.

Quinn also had little doubt that one of the strike team's final acts before extracting from the hit zone would be to put a burst into him, as well. Quinn had seen their faces, heard their voices, observed their tactics.

He had told them that he was a vacationing American relative of the Frenchman, and in their haste they had bought his story, or chose not to attach high priority to it when Quinn produced flash ID under another name, insisting that he had lost his passport. Actually, he hoped that his passport was still in his office safe back in the States.

Quinn had put on a servile front, counting on it to cause his captors to drop their guard at a critical moment.

From the minor indulgences they were showing him, Quinn judged the tactic to be working. They considered that their victim was scared witless and they expected he would do whatever they wanted him to do, even believing their empty promise to leave him unharmed as long as he cooperated.

This was a basic tenet of hostage-taking psychology and one Quinn was counting on his captors to take for granted, since it played to their own psychological needs to believe that they were in total control of the operational environment at all times and were superior to those they hunted and killed.

He would use this factor as a countermanipulation gambit in order to turn the tables on the hostage takers.

"Walk normally but don't stray too far or you'll catch a bullet," Skate gruffly told Quinn, nudging him forward. "In this confusion you'll drop right away, and we'll be long gone before anyone realizes you've been shot. Nod if you understand."

Quinn nodded, simulating a slight tremble.

"Very good. What we'll do now is take in the local color. We'll recognize Thibodeaux—we know what he looks like. When we spot him, you are to wave to the Frenchman and walk toward his position. Remember, we have no beef with you. When we've dealt with Thibodeaux, we'll cut you loose."

Quinn nodded again as he followed Skate's instructions and walked along the length of the parade flotilla, which was moving up the boulevard.

As one of the pageant's grand marshals, Thibodeaux would be somewhere at the head of the flotilla.

Quinn made his way toward the front of the procession of parade floats, multicolored confetti raining down on himself and his three companions, the man and woman flanking him to left and right while Skate stayed glued to his back with a machine pistol thrust into his kidneys.

Before too long the foursome came abreast of the main float.

Now Quinn could see the Frenchman standing on it, dressed as Humpty Dumpty with a huge papier-mâché egg hanging on suspenders from his shoulders and a stovepipe hat perched atop his bald head as he waved to the crowds below.

Rodriguez was beside Thibodeaux, and Quinn could not suppress a smile as he saw the bikini-clad island beauties his friend clutched around the waist in each hand as they poured champagne into his mouth from a black bottle.

"Easy now," the woman beside Quinn said as they approached the float and she recognized the Frenchman, too. "Do as you're told and you won't get hurt. When you see Thibodeaux, wave to him and slowly walk toward the float."

As Quinn came to the front of the slowly moving parade float, Thibodeaux and Rodriguez both caught sight of him. He heard the Frenchman call out to him while Rodriguez grabbed the champagne bottle from one of the women and held it aloft, spilling the bubbly over himself and the girls while gesturing with the bottle for Quinn to join the party.

"Now," Emerald rasped in his ear while she put on a show of smiling up at the Frenchman. "Wave to him. Smile when you do it."

Quinn stopped short, still feeling the gun muzzle in his back, and raised his right arm in a gesture of greeting.

He never completed the gesture.

While his arm was at eye level, deliberately pivoting his body slightly, Quinn felt the pressure of iron against his flesh momentarily ease, then disappear entirely. He knew that the gun was no longer pointing directly at his vitals.

Continuing to wave and turn his body, Quinn pivoted suddenly on his right foot and lashed out at Skate's gun hand with a savage blow to the wrist delivered with the hardened edge of his hand.

Skate cursed in sudden pain as the autopistol flew from his grasp, but he was quickly dropped by Quinn's knee smashing into his testicles. He sank to the street, moaning and feeling hot tears well up in his eyes.

While this was going down, Emerald and Trident whipped out their weapons from the concealment of their jackets and brought the double-action 9 mm subguns into firing position, both a trigger pull away from unleashing stuttering lances of lethal steel.

Their line of sight was not good, though, and they were forced to waste critical seconds before opening up as half-naked revelers passed in front of them, too drunk to grasp the seriousness of what was happening.

Quinn used those vital seconds to bring the gun he'd taken from Skate up to the temple of the nearest gunman, Trident, and pump three rounds into his face at point-blank range.

Flame scorched his flesh as metal rivets punched into his brain, and Trident's head caved in as a massive exit wound spewed interior matter all over some unlucky revelers who were now running en masse from the strike scene.

Emerald was left standing, but the woman was quick and she was dangerous. She leaped, cat-like atop the parade float and leveled a Spectre burst at Thibodeaux, who ducked for cover.

By this time Quinn brought up the autopistol and unleashed most of its remaining ammo reserves at her just as she was about to fire at the Frenchman again. She dropped to the pavement to lie in a twisted heap, blood staining her red hair and pulsing in dark jets from her ruptured throat.

Recovering from where he was sprawled a short distance away, Skate saw the dully glinting black Spectre that had fallen from Trident's hands. He lunged at the SMG and grasped its butt in his hand. Skate had a new respect for the man they had taken hostage at the Frenchman's house. He had expertly conned them into believing he was a rich, weak punk when in fact he was something entirely different.

"Watch it!" shouted Rodriguez as Quinn turned to face the surviving, and most danger-ous, member of the strike team. "He's got a gun!"

Skate then did the only thing possible: he grabbed a hostage.

Minutes before, the woman had looked like a scarlet flower as she gyrated to the beat of hot calypso music in her skimpy red costume.

Now terror gripped her as the executioner's fingers grasped her arm with steel-torsioned strength, and the muzzle of his gun pressed painfully into the side of her neck.

"Toss the weapon aside," Skate growled at Quinn, who hesitated for a moment. Skate shouted his command again, pulling the woman closer to himself. "Now."

Quinn let the Mauser slip from his fingers, and it clattered hollowly to the street.

"Drop down," Skate demanded. "Get on with it or I'll pull the trigger."

Quinn did as ordered while Skate dragged his screaming captive through the crowd. Adrenaline was making him sweat profusely, and the moisture-saturated tropical air increased the already shattering tension he felt.

Sweat poured down the front of his colorfully patterned shirt now, staining it in huge, dark patches, and soaked his hair, making it stand away from his scalp.

Although there were police cars now parked on the fringes of the crowd, their circus lights flashing, Skate knew there was no using them for a getaway.

The merc game had few hard and fast rules, but one of those few was this: never take an assignment on an island. Islands were like Venus flytraps—easy to get into, damn near impossible to get out when the going got rough.

Skate had at first declined to accept the contract for this reason, but the Belgian gunrunners who had put together the strike had made him an offer he couldn't refuse.

The down payment sitting in his numbered Swiss account was a quarter of a million with an equal sum stipulated as a bonus on completion of the mission. Skate cursed himself now for having taken the seductive bait.

Because of the big bucks and the high quality of the mission-support infrastructure, as well as the promise of a quick in-and-out strike, he had allowed himself to be blinded to the hazards of the run.

He had intended to retire after this one, with the proceeds from the assignment. Having been dazzled by his own greed, he felt like a twice-damned fool.

No, there was no point in grabbing a police vehicle. He wouldn't get anywhere on this island shithole.

Skate would have to disappear somehow and arrange passage off the island. The crowds, which had initially promised an easy getaway from the hit zone, were now a severe liability. A thousand eyes watched the drama unfold, each pair a witness to his crimes.

Skate would first need to get out of the limelight, into the darkness of the surrounding back streets and from there into the remote sections of the island.

If he could steal or rent a boat, he might have a chance.

There were hundreds of coves in the island complex; smugglers and pirates had been using them as hideouts for centuries.

Having dragged the woman from the edge of the crowd, Skate saw the narrow alleyways stretching away from the thoroughfare.

It was time to play his hole card.

The whimpering woman had served her purpose. Giving her a hard shove, Skate sent her sprawling to the street and pulled a flash-bang from his pocket. He pitched the stun grenade, then turned and darted into one of the alleys nearby as the flash-bang gave off blinding light and deafening blast effect, screening him from view as he disappeared into the twisting, shadowy maze of back streets.

23

Already on his feet, Quinn scanned the melee from his position near the parade float after Skate had taken off. After a moment he heard the flash-bang go off a short distance away. The strobing flashes and sharp, hammering blasts and the screams of revelers thrown into a panic by the grenade burst came from the main thoroughfare somewhere to his right.

Grabbing the Spectre submachine gun dropped by Emerald, Quinn turned to Rodriguez, who still stood atop the float beside Thibodeaux. The portly French arms dealer wore a stunned expression on his face, looking pathetic in his carnival suit.

"I'm going after him," he told his friend.

"I'm with you, partner," Rodriguez returned, making to jump down from the float.

"Negative," Quinn countered. "You stay with Thibodeaux. We don't know if there's backup. See that he gets safely back to the villa."

"Yeah, guess you're right," Rodriguez told Quinn after a moment of consideration. "Good hunting."

Quinn shoved his way through the milling ranks of frightened partiers and soon reached the site of the flash-bang explosion. It was marked by the spent submunition casing and the crowd of people stumbling around in a daze, the after-effects of being exposed to a burst from a disrupter grenade.

Managing to glean from several of the disoriented bystanders that Skate had gone into the mouth of a narrow alleyway a few feet away, Quinn followed the fleeing merc's path. He picked up Skate as the merc was sprinting into a street-level doorway he'd just kicked open.

Quinn followed the fleeing merc into the building. Sighting Quinn, Skate wheeled abruptly, leveling the Spectre in his fist, and launched a multiround burst of parabellum steel at Quinn, forcing him to break for cover around the corner as bullets spanged off the iron door frame, fragmenting dangerously.

Quinn was back inside the entranceway a moment later, seeing sneakered feet pounding up the stairs, and Quinn followed the running gunman, determined to take him at all costs.

Reaching the top of the landing, Skate stood beneath a skylight and beside a padlocked iron door leading to the roof. Behind him he could hear Quinn's racing footsteps on the stairs.

Skate shot off the lock and bounded onto the flat roof of the low-rise building. Quinn reached the swinging door a few moments later and went through it, breaking left on a half roll.

Evading the Spectre fire Skate snapped off, Quinn flattened himself around the corner of the large concrete chimney stack to his right.

Counting out three beats, then darting sideways with his own Spectre primed to fire, he saw Skate already making a break for the edge of the roof.

Quinn decided not to throw steel at the hunched silhouette.

His ammo reserves were uncertain, and he wanted as good a chance to hit the merc as he could obtain. Visibility in the darkness was poor, and Skate was already out of the killbox.

Reaching the edge of the roof, Skate took a running jump across the narrow alley separating the rooftop from the top of the building beside it. Having broken from cover, Quinn followed the fleeing hitman, executing the leap across the narrow alley with ease.

On the adjacent rooftop, Skate wheeled in place and fired again, forcing Quinn to hunker down behind the rooftop entrance. Quinn saw the shadow figure skylighted against the indigo horizon as he broad-jumped yet another alley and landed on another roof.

Once more Skate fired, but the Spectre's bolt action locked after only two rounds were discharged. The weapon's clip was empty, and Skate had no reloads.

He flung the now-useless weapon at Quinn, who cut loose with a burst of the Spectre in his fists, sending slugs digging into the rooftop as Skate turned and fled.

The bolt of Quinn's double-action SITES SMG also locked in place as the last shell casing was ejected: Quinn had depleted his own ammo reserves just as had his quarry.

Jettisoning the SMG and giving chase, Quinn caught up with Skate as he ducked over the edge of the roof and began descending a fire escape fronting a large, blazing neon sign advertising Cayman Cola in luminous reds, greens and yellows.

Quinn jumped onto the platform of steel slats, knocking Skate down in the process.

Skate recovered from the assault with surprising agility and launched a series of martial arts kicks at Quinn, who soft-blocked the blows and countered with a series of spinning reverse snap kicks that scored successive hits on Skate's midsection.

Skate went down but sprang back up to lash out at Quinn with hooked finger strikes that slashed across his face, opening up a huge bleeding gash along his temple. Quinn countered the assaults with a pounding series of rapid back-fist blows, but Skate fended them off with arm and foot blocks and managed to counterattack with a side kick to Quinn's chest, which sent him reeling perilously close to the platform's edge.

Regaining his balance again, Quinn grabbed at Skate's boot heels as he tried to climb back up the fire escape, but the merc lashed out savagely, kicking Quinn in his wounded head, and scrambled over the side of the roof.

Skate smelled the odor of freshly laid tar, saw the long wooden broom handle sticking up out of a black can sitting over near the housing of the rooftop entranceway. He ran over to the can and pulled out the handle, quickly unscrewing the tar-sticky brush.

Clutching the makeshift stick weapon, Skate began swinging it back and forth with blinding speed and deadly precision in a series of *hapkido*-style moves as Quinn gained the rooftop behind him.

Quinn dodged the expertly executed blows as Skate took the offensive with the fighting stick. Quinn knew that although Skate was winded, he was still plenty dangerous.

Skate's strategy was working.

As Quinn struggled to stay out of the way of the punishing strikes, Skate was steadily backing him up toward the edge of the rooftop.

Holding the stick to one side in a double-handed grip, Skate immediately shifted strategy from delivering edge-on swipes to executing straightforward thrusts with the doweled end of the stick aimed at Quinn's most-vulnerable body zones while Quinn used foot and hand blocks to deflect the increasingly dangerous and increasingly accurate strikes.

Expertly timing his countermoves, Quinn succeeded in catching the end of the stick inside the crook of his arm while simultaneously following through with an edged hand blow delivered to the side of Skate's face.

Dazed, Skate relaxed his grip on the weapon. His hands would be effectively pinned if he didn't release the stick, but Skate reflexively continued to hold on to the weapon.

That turned out to be a fatal mistake as Quinn struck Skate another stunning head blow and used the leverage of his grasp on the stick to pivot Skate sharply around.

Skate stumbled into the edge of the low parapet encircling the rooftop and lost his footing.

With a scream he went tumbling over the edge of the roof to plummet three stories to the alley below. Tossing the stick to the rooftop, where it fell with a clatter, Quinn looked over the edge and saw that Skate lay facedown on the pavement, looking as dead as they came.

BACK BY THE PARADE FLOAT, police sirens were wailing as more vehicles arrived on the scene.

Doors on patrol cars slammed, and soon uniformed local police were elbowing their way through the thick of the rubberneckers to approach the site of the shootings.

The Frenchman was already negotiating with the officers, however, and Rodriguez saw clearly that Thibodeaux, with his personal connections, would have no difficulty in ensuring that the matter was quickly taken care of and that the parade could resume.

But another car screeched up to the parade scene moments later. The Frenchman and the alligator hunter saw a man in a white tropical suit emerge and flash identification at one of the officers who was standing around a hastily improvised cordon keeping the curious at bay.

Neither Rodriguez nor Thibodeaux recognized the man with lank sand-colored hair who had stepped from the car and was now walking toward them.

It was Lorimer, and he was looking for Quinn.

24

The border town was picturesque, at least by American standards. It was a town already old by the time of the Swedish invasion of Finland in the twelfth century, with medieval streets built on hillsides and narrow alleys lined with touristy shops.

The local color was completely lost on Griffin, however. The cybernetically augmented parahuman had other priorities: Viipuri, formerly Vyborg, was situated on Russia's northern border. Adjacent to an important crossing point from Europe since being ceded to Finland decades before, it was about five hundred miles to Moscow, and much less to St. Petersburg.

Since his arrival only a few hours earlier, Griffin had been subjecting the local Finns to IVD scans for the precise match he required.

When he chanced upon Arvo Kekonnen emerging from a local liquor store with a bottle tucked under his arm, Griffin knew he had at last found the individual he required.

Griffin followed Kekonnen down zigzagging streets to a small carpenter's shop tucked away on a narrow side street that branched off from a small town square with a fountain at its center.

Scanning the square, Griffin waited until an elderly couple emerged from the side street his quarry had taken, then he crossed the plaza and walked down the narrow cobblestone street that ran along the side of the shop.

The alley made a sudden turn not far from the window of the carpenter's shop. Griffin followed it and found the rear door of the shop just around a dogleg bend.

On trying the door, he discovered that it was locked from the inside, but a twist of the doorknob with Griffin's steel-taloned right hand ripped both the knob and the innards of the lock clean out of the door in a second flat.

Griffin stepped into the heated room beyond, smelling the odor of various woods and oils used in the carpenter's trade. As he silently stalked his prey, Griffin heard the cadence of steady hammering.

It came from the workshop located at the store's front, and the blows of the hammer sounded almost in time to the beat of a popular song with Finnish lyrics coming from a portable stereo set.

Kekonnen looked up, the mallet in his hand frozen in midswing as he saw the stranger enter the room. Believing the intruder to be a thief, Kekonnen raised the mallet he'd been hammering nails with and charged Griffin with his eyes wide and a bellow of rage on his lips.

Kekonnen was muscular and an ex-wrestler; indeed, it was for his physical resemblance to Griffin that the clone had selected him to be his victim.

As Kekonnen charged at the intruder like the angry bull that he resembled, he swung the hammer at Griffin's head, intending to brain him and let the police sort out the details after the fact.

Nobody had a right to break into his shop. He would make the intruder pay dearly for his temerity.

Griffin's hand shot up and grasped Kekonnen's wrist, halting the sweep of the mallet in midswing. Kekonnen's eyes bulged in his face as he strained to pull his hand free of the powerful grasp, but he was pinioned in place as securely as a dowel of wood in the jaws of one of the vises on his workbench.

The former wrestler was suddenly afraid.

Even in a test of strength between the most powerful opponents, there was always give and take, the sense of struggling against flesh and sinew.

Here there was none of that.

The intruder's grasp did not give an inch, no matter how hard Kekonnen struggled. It was as if his hand had suddenly become frozen in a block of stone.

Reaching out with his free hand, Griffin picked the man up like a rag doll and dashed him against the floor full force. Kekonnen landed with a crash, his spine broken and blood pouring out of the back of his skull.

Paralyzed and losing consciousness, he lay on the floor moaning as Griffin took the mallet from his hand and slammed it down against the bridge of his nose, caving in his skull with a single blow and obliterating the delicate brain matter inside the cage of bone.

Not too long afterward Griffin was driving Kekonnen's Volvo toward the border crossing with Finland's enormous southern neighbor, Russia.

Programmed to speak sixty languages, including Russian and the various Slavic tongues of Eastern Europe, Griffin bantered easily with the border guards as they looked over Kekonnen's driver's license and identity papers and passed him through.

A few minutes later Griffin was across the border in Russian territory, and only four hundred fifty miles from Moscow Center itself.

Griffin followed the directional signs posted at intervals along the highway until he reached the city of St. Petersburg. There he repeated the process by which he had gained Finnish identity to equip himself with Russian identity papers, money and a new car, this time an ancient Zhiguli sedan with a sticky transmission and backfiring exhaust system.

The car proved sufficient to carry him the remaining distance to Moscow, where Griffin parked it on a side street and went the rest of the way on foot until he reached an entrance to the extensive Moscow subway system—a system almost as large as New York's with its hundreds of miles of track.

Using his newfound rubles to pay his fare, Griffin rode the Moscow subway until he found a deserted station.

Once there, he jumped from the platform and proceeded the rest of the way along the tracks, his internal light amplification system clearly showing him the way through the inky darkness.

Before long the subway tracks branched off onto a side tunnel which, unlike the main tunnel from which he had come, was completely unlit.

Inside the tunnel Griffin's IVD scan showed piles of unused construction equipment and heaps of sandbags. Judging by the layer of dust covering them, they had not been touched for a very long time.

It was beneath the pile of sandbags that Griffin hid the first of his two powerful nuclear bombs. Bombs that were small enough to remain undetected for an indefinite time yet were powerful enough to vaporize the heart of downtown Moscow.

MISSION LOG THREE:

Shock Wave

25

The faint ozone smell of electrostatically scrubbed air filled the space-age crypt. The module was well lit now by sterile overhead light panels.

Quinn and Lorimer walked through it in the eerie silence, examining the place where Griffin had been housed for over a decade in his cybernetically-controlled and drug-induced hallucinatory coma at the behest of the soulless bureaucrats, mad scientists and faceless Intelligence planners who had cloned him from the body cells of another man, replaced selected pieces of flesh and bone with silicon and metal and trained him to kill in the name of global peace.

In the center of the sterile white chamber was a clear Plexiglas cocoon. Split hemispherically, its hatch was now canted at an angle and held up by pneumatically controlled pistons. Quinn walked over to the cyberpod and looked inside, taking note of the gray platform in its center on which Griffin had lain in his long artificial sleep.

Made of the same material as the cushion Quinn had become acquainted with at the euthanasia center in Las Vegas, the slab bore the contours it had "remembered" as belonging to the former occupant of the sleep cocoon.

A multiheaded hydra of cables snaked from conduits attached to the slab, some of them tipped with sensor pads, others with the blunt stainless-steel snouts of pneumatic injector nodes.

"Hard to imagine being stuck in that thing," Lorimer said to Quinn as he, too, inspected the cocoon. "But paradoxically this chamber is one of the safest places in the world, hardened against every possible contingency from natural disaster to nuclear war."

"It must have cost millions," Quinn ventured.

"Billions," Lorimer corrected. "At least, it would have run to seven figures over the long haul. As far as Griffin himself was concerned, he could count on emerging from the cocoon scarcely a day older than when he had entered. Some of the intravenous drugs reduced his metabolism and bodily functions to the point where only the faintest vital processes took place. Heartbeat and pulse were slowed to a crawl, breathing was minimal. Feeding was intravenous, too, and eliminated matter was shunted off and then chemically disposed of.''

Quinn turned his attention from the cyberpod and inspected the few other objects in the sterile chamber.

These were banks of computers monitoring the occupant of the module, tanks containing drugs and nutrients that the computers controlled and arrays of video cameras and other sensing devices needed to keep constant tabs on what took place at the installation.

''All of this to keep a single man alive, for what?'' Quinn asked Lorimer.

''Griffin wasn't just a man,'' the agent answered. ''He was a weapon, the end product of decades of experimentation, and he represented an investment of an astronomical sum in research-and-development costs. I don't completely agree with the logic of how it went down, but to destroy the prototype of a weapons system of such magnitude might have deprived the nation of it in time of war. What if the Russians or some other power unleashed an army of 'Griffins' on us? What then?'' Lorimer asked.

"I'm sorry to say it, but the end usually justifies the means where defense is concerned."

"Not to me, it doesn't," Quinn responded. "We're a violent species. Killing is in our genes, and it would be naive to think we'll ever stop. But we've learned something in over five million years of evolution, Lorimer, and that is that our species has to draw the line somewhere, has to put the brakes on devising new and more-efficient methods of murdering ourselves if we're to survive on this planet. To build something like Griffin is, in the long run, to commit global suicide."

"We'll visit the control hub next," Lorimer told Quinn, averting his gaze, coloring slightly in embarrassment. "It's a couple of miles from this installation."

"You say that it controls several of these cybernetic—these cyberpods?" Quinn asked.

"That's right," Lorimer affirmed. "They're scattered across the tristate area and well hidden. Some are individual pods, others house several clone prototypes, all less advanced than Griffin and none of them as heavily armored or cybernetically augmented. The entire number of clones still kept under storage is classified, I'm afraid."

"My advice to you is to bail out of the Agency, Lorimer," Quinn said. "If and when this ever becomes public, the soulless bastards you work for are going to have a lot of explaining to do."

"I don't have to remind you that you signed a secrecy oath before we began, Quinn," Lorimer said, his jaw tensing.

"I remember," Quinn replied angrily. "And I've seen enough here. Let's have a look at the control hub of the system."

After a short drive across desert roads, Lorimer and Quinn were admitted to a high-security complex enclosed by a tall perimeter fence.

Only a few concrete blockhouses were visible on the surface. The control hub of the pod network was buried deep below ground. The installation housed DARPA research facilities and extended for at least a square mile beneath the earth.

Quinn and Lorimer were escorted through the base by a balding, middle-aged man with a bland, fleshy face who introduced himself as the chief systems officer.

"I'm Braithwaite," he said to the visitors as they approached the door to the main systems node. The beam of a low-intensity laser wrapped itself around Braithwaite's face, and scanners set in the wall matched retinal, blood vessel and voice patterns against an ID template in computer memory.

The door slid open with a pneumatic hiss, admitting the chief tech and his two visitors into a square-sided chamber crammed with computer equipment.

"Is this Barasheens's station?" Quinn asked, indicating a console dominated by banks of raster screens displaying blanking patterns of idling video computer processing units.

"That's correct," Braithwaite responded coldly, obviously peeved at having intruders come into what he considered his private domain. When Quinn seated himself in front of the console and began inputting code at the keyboard, he added, "If you're thinking of finding anything of importance there, it's only fair to tell you that I personally supervised a full-security scan of the system and found nothing."

"Thanks for telling me," Quinn replied absentmindedly, already absorbed in entering the system. While Braithwaite and Lorimer watched—Braithwaite with a superior smirk on his face as his eyes were glued to the code sequences that Quinn was entering at the keyboard—the screens winked to life and a progression of constantly changing data streamed across them.

Minutes passed without anyone speaking until a text block appeared. It read, "A statement in my own defense, Technician Dexter Barasheens. Press any key to proceed."

"Did you come across this batch file?" Quinn asked Braithwaite, turning from the screen for a moment.

"No," Braithwaite responded, not smiling anymore. "This...this is completely unfamiliar."

"I'm not surprised," Quinn said. "Let's see what else there is." He hit the space bar, and a prompt appeared, asking Quinn to enter the date and time.

Then another prompt asked, "Enter whereabouts of Dexter Barasheens."

Quinn typed in: "Deceased."

"Thank you," the message came on-screen. "Confirmed. Stand by for statement of 3998 K-bytes in length."

Quinn hit the command for a hard printout as the screen was filled with text.

Since this file has been accessed, I must presume that I have shuffled off my mortal coil. I suspected that such a risk existed from the outset, and so have taken the precaution of recording what little I've learned about the events which have led to this final development.

Let me preface my statement by saying that I am a loyal American and as concerned as the next man about the welfare of my country and the world. That having been said, I add that there are some issues that any individual must, in good conscience, stand contra.

The project code-named Upcard is one of those. Since beginning my assignment at the complex, I have spent long hours pondering the fact that I am the custodian of what must be the most barbaric corruption of science in the history of mankind. The monstrosity lying dormant in the chamber has been stripped of basic human dignity, which resides in man's innate ability to feel a kinship with his fellow man. To use such a creature as a weapon is unconscionable. Yet I would not have acted as I did without a catalyst.

The spark came one night at the Penguin Lounge, a nearby bar featuring exotic dancers. One night I was approached by a woman who identified herself as Joan King and asked if I would buy her a drink. I did. She was very nice to me. Far too nice to a man who has never had much luck with women before. We dated. As she asked me questions about my work, I began to understand that she was a recruiter. For whom I did not know, although in time I surmised that it would be the Russians or the Japanese.

Ultimately the expected took place: she asked me if I would be willing to meet with someone who could pay me a great deal of money for a job I could perform. I agreed to the meeting. We were joined at the Penguin Lounge by an individual who identified himself as Arthur Scoville. Scoville told me point-blank that he wanted me to release the clone.

I initially refused, but then began to reexamine my thinking. If the clone were released, the obscenity committed in the name of justifiable ends would be revealed to the world. It didn't matter who was responsible for it—in the end it would all come out the same. I agreed to release the clone, receiving the sum of a hundred thousand dollars,

which I considered fair compensation for
the fact that I would no longer be employ-
able after committing a breach of federal
law. I do not regret having done what I did,
only the manner in which its outcome affected me personally.

However, I have one final surprise for you
all. Despite my good friend and associate
Martin Braithwaite's careful scrutiny of the
system, he has neglected to locate a hidden
virus I have planted in the boot sector of the
system's master disk. By the time you fin-
ish reading this sentence, the virus will have
caused not only a massive system crash but
the explosion of the entire stinking—

Braithwaite was already running for the door.
Expecting the imminent explosion promised by
the software, he was frantically trying to insert
his card key into its slot to unlock it. Quinn,
however, showed no sign of agitation. In fact, he
smiled as he turned toward Braithwaite.

"Relax," Quinn told the chief systems officer. "I suspected there'd be a second turn of the
screw in the works someplace. With a man like
Barasheens, that's only prudent."

Braithwaite looked around him, wild-eyed and
high on his own adrenaline, unsure if the complex were going to blow or not. Sweat beaded his

forehead as he slumped against a wall and wiped at his brow with a handkerchief as his pulse rate began to slow again and his breathing grew steadier.

"How the hell did you know?" he asked hoarsely. "How the hell? I personally went over every byte of data. I personally—"

"It's like this," Quinn said, cutting him off. "As you know, systems designers always leave themselves 'back doors,' holes in the system through which they can sneak to correct a bug or track down the evidence of a cracker's handiwork."

"Yes, of course that's true," Braithwaite responded. "But I still—"

"Barasheens turned the game around," Quinn interjected. "He created false 'back doors,' or holes in the system that led nowhere. The real ones were constantly aliasing themselves so you couldn't track them conventionally. I started out looking for aliased files. But I also wondered what other mayhem a troubled mind like Barasheens's would concoct.

"The software 'bomb' he planted was both a literal and figurative one. It would have overloaded the mainframe's power supply and caused a massive blowout. I've neutralized it, as you can see, although I suggest doing a complete shutdown until I personally have had a chance to go over the system."

Braithwaite colored now, anger doing to his vital signs what fear had done a few minutes before.

"You son of a bitch," he cursed softly.

By that time, however, Quinn and Lorimer had already left the control room. Lorimer would recommend that Braithwaite have a complete psychological workup before being allowed to return to his post. He was obviously a man under a great deal of stress.

"YEAH, I KNOW THAT GUY," the owner of the Penguin Lounge said as Lorimer showed him an identikit hologram of the man who Barasheens had described and named as Arthur Scoville. "He used to come in here a lot, and frequently with the woman."

"You said 'used to,'" Lorimer went on. "What's that mean, exactly?"

"Means just what I said," the owner replied, looking at Lorimer as though he were an imbecile. "Guy's not coming around anymore. Hasn't been around in, let's see, three, four weeks at least. Same goes for the woman. Now, if you gentlemen don't mind, I got a place to run."

Outside, Lorimer drove while Quinn rode the shotgun seat.

"Likeable guy," Lorimer ventured. "Here comes the data on our friend Scoville."

Beneath the dashboard the cellular fax machine was spitting out a color reproduction of the individual depicted in the identikit holo. At the same time the dashboard viewscreen showed a holographic image of the subject.

"Arthur Scoville. Real name—Valentin Ionescu," the artificial female voice said from the dash speaker. "Age forty-five. Nationality—Romanian, son of a Securitate chief ousted in the revolution of 1989. Current whereabouts unknown. Ionescu has been a field asset freelancing his services for various global paymasters both in the government and private sector. He was instrumental in obtaining illegal transfer of technology to the Japanese. Believed to be under KGB contract most recently," concluded the computer voice.

Lorimer logged in his recommendation for an immediate search to be instituted for Ionescu and the female agent now known to be one Joan DeKeyser, with whom he had engineered several "honey traps" for recruitment purposes.

Neither Quinn nor the Company man believed that either of the two could tell them anything substantially more than they already knew. For that they would need to talk directly with their Russian counterparts.

26

The aircraft began its descent at the edge of
space. Gliding down from the blackness of the
upper stratosphere, the sleek-nosed, adaptable-
wing aerospace plane slowed from its scramjet-
powered cruising speed of Mach 25 to the slower
speeds of a conventional supersonic jet as it began burning the denser mix of oxygen, nitrogen
and carbon dioxide of the lower atmosphere.

Soon passengers who glanced up from their in-
flight interactive videos and out of their virtual
reality Mind Blaster eyephones could see the sky
turn cobalt and slowly fade to a vibrant and
more-familiar blue coloration just beyond their
windows.

Quinn and Lorimer sat in the first-class compartment at the front of the plane. They had
spent the past hour of the two-hour flight from
Moscow to Washington discussing the information that their KGB liaison had revealed to them.

The crisis, they realized, was far greater now
since the Russians had revealed their suspicions
to the Americans during a series of secret meet-

ings at the dacha of the Komitet's director, Boris Afanasiev, outside of Moscow.

The U.S. President's ARGUS initiative was more than a plan at this stage.

The Russians had shown them incontrovertible Intelligence telling the visitors that it was in fact a reality, and they were fuming at having been co-opted in such a cavalier fashion.

"You Americans never change," Afanasiev, a tall, bearded figure had yelled at one point, pounding his fist on the desktop. "Peace, peace, peace you talk while you prepare to stab whoever is stupid enough to believe you in the back. Now you may have doomed the entire world with your imbecilic and bullheaded unilateral defense initiative."

This flew in the face of the President's insistence that ARGUS did not yet exist and the media's postulating that ARGUS was a disinformation tactic of the same kind as the so-called Star Wars antinuclear shield during the Reagan Presidency of the early eighties had been, a tactic for wringing additional disarmament concessions from the Soviets, who had balked at further cuts in their missiles since the START agreement of the early nineties.

The installation of the ARGUS infrastructure was already in position.

Documentary evidence from unimpeachable sources had clearly demonstrated that the network of land- sea- and space-based sensors linked to high-radiation-yield plutonium bombs in secret installations did in fact exist and was already fully operational.

The machinery for rendering all life on the planet obsolete was fully in place, and the only conclusion that could be drawn was that some unknown chain of events in the White House policy-making process had put it there.

From what the KGB had been able to piece together, the late Colonel Sergei Korniyenko and a cadre of Komitet and GRU hard-liners intent on undermining the President's efforts to install the ARGUS system had been determined to use the warrior clone code-named Griffin to discredit him.

But the parahuman had long ago ceased to be accountable to his handlers in Moscow Center.

He was acting autonomously.

Again, the preponderance of the Intelligence data had been overwhelming. There was no doubt that Griffin was a loose cannon. There was no question that Griffin was engaged in a deliberate plan of his own, and the suspicion had been growing: did this plan include ARGUS?

Afanasiev's words still rang in Quinn's mind. "If it does," the KGB director had insisted, "then the blood of billions will be on your President's hands!"

As the ASP—aerospace plane—bearing Quinn and Lorimer descended from orbit to make its final descent before landing at Dulles International Airport, the object of their concern was several thousand feet below them, walking down a ramp of the airport parking garage.

Having monitored the opposition's efforts to apprehend him via cracking computer data bases, Griffin had been aware of Quinn's having joined the worldwide hunt for him.

He had learned, too, that Quinn had been his clonal parent, having been explanted to donate the tissue from which Griffin had been grown in vitro.

The new knowledge of Quinn's identity meant nothing to Griffin. He did not consider Quinn to be his father, his brother or any other form of natural kin. To Griffin there were only two kinds of people: controllers and targets. Quinn was now one of the latter.

More than anything else, Quinn was a wild card to Griffin, representing the potential of interference with his plan. Quinn's thoughts were Griffin's thoughts; Quinn's persona was Griffin's persona.

Out of the ten billion humans who inhabited the planet, Quinn was the single individual who could anticipate Griffin's actions. Termination of Quinn had therefore always been a mission priority, although not an especially pressing one, since the Agency's hunt for Quinn had taken the heat off Griffin.

Until now, that is.

Griffin knew that Quinn had ceased to be hunted in his place. Instead, his clonal parent was actively seeking him out, bent on his destruction.

Griffin knew, too, that he had visited the site of the cyberpod and that he had pieced together a possible link with ARGUS. Before long he would come to grasp the entirety of Griffin's objective and might well be in a position to prevent him from fulfilling his carefully laid plans.

Now that a judgment call was imminent, Griffin wondered if he had deliberately held back in hitting Quinn. Had he really delayed because it was not operationally viable?

Or was there another reason?

Quinn was a target, nothing more. There was no possibility, not even a remote one, of anything resembling feeling entering into the decision-making loop.

Griffin was incapable of turning philosophical abstractions into impediments to direct, violent action. That had been programmed out of him. Which is where he differed from Quinn, as he did from all other ordinary men—the submen.

Griffin felt no kinship with the submen. They had provided the raw genetic material from which his kind had been created, yes. But the relationship began and ended there.

Griffin's true peers were the other subjects of Upcard, clones that he knew were still in cold storage at various facilities across the country. Griffin would free them, and when he did, he would rule over them as they would in turn rule the submen.

He was getting ahead of himself, though. This eventuality was still some time away. Right now he had other more immediate concerns to deal with. Taking care of Quinn, for one thing.

Griffin walked into the terminal building and checked the departure and arrival schedules posted on large wall displays, noting that the next

Aeroflot flight in from Moscow was due to arrive in twenty minutes.

This provided plenty of time for Griffin to get into place, but he did not want to be seen or photographed spending too much time in the arrivals lounge. Airports were areas that were kept under constant surveillance, and Griffin was the object of a worldwide hunt.

Griffin walked down the mall area lined on both sides with shops selling everything from souvenirs to designer drugs. He decided on the bar a few shop fronts down and to his right and walked into the dimly lit lounge.

Taking a seat at the bar, he stared at the holographic flat-screen TV on which a baseball game was taking place.

"What's your pleasure?" asked the bartender.

"My pleasure?" Griffin repeated.

"Yeah, your pleasure," the bartender replied, flashing Griffin a look reserved for dimwits. He waited a beat while Griffin stared at him with a peculiar blank expression. "You want a drink, pal, or don't you?" asked the bartender.

"Yes," replied Griffin. "I want a drink. Give me one please."

"Well, we got that out of the way, pal," the bartender said. "Now what kind of a drink do you want?" he went on to ask.

Other patrons had started to take notice of the exchange, and Griffin didn't like the attention he was suddenly getting. He had come into the bar to escape notice, not to attract it.

Griffin pointed to one of the bottles in back of the bartender. The bartender turned. "Okay, pal, one Stolichnaya pertsovka, coming up. You want it on the rocks?"

"No," Griffin replied. "I'll drink it here."

The bartender paused and looked into Griffin's eyes, getting hot under the collar. However, one glance into those bottomless gray orbs told him that he wasn't dealing with a guy who had his head on straight. The bartender poured the pertsovka, anxious to collect the bar tab and quickly take care of another patron.

"That'll be twenty bucks," he said, watching the customer inspect the roll of bills he'd taken from his pocket as though looking at money for the first time. "Thanks, pal," he said, and moved to the register, watching out of the corner of his eye as the crazy man raised the glass to his lips and drained it in a single swallow.

Griffin sat at the bar and noticed that some of the other patrons were idly eating nuts and pretzels taken from small baskets as they watched the holo.

Griffin did the same, munching the mix as he looked at the TV, wondering why the warriors stationed in the field did not use lethal force when one swung the wooden weapon and hit the small, round, incoming projectile.

Soon, however, a flashing green blip appeared in his internal visual display as Griffin's on-board computer began a two-minute countdown to the arrival of the target plane.

Griffin promptly got up from the stool and began walking toward the door and into the crowded terminal lobby.

Just as he was walking out, a seven-foot, four-hundred-pound wrestler named Cosmo the Cosmic, connecting at Dulles for a flight to Dubuque, pushed in through the door.

Griffin walked right into him and sent Cosmo flying out into the terminal, where he landed on his behind. Cosmo shook his head as he looked up at the guy who had bumped him, wondering if he had been hit by a tank.

"Pardon me," Griffin said, and walked on through the terminal.

27

Thanks to Lorimer's CIA identification, he and Quinn breezed through customs and were out in the airport's spacious arrivals lounge in minutes. As a general rule, arrivals lounges were usually jammed with an assortment of people, and the one at Dulles was no exception.

Conscious of the resentful glances shot their way by other passengers who had to wait in long lines before passing through customs, Quinn and Lorimer left the area via a wide corridor that brought them into the packed central terminal area where passengers from a dozen flights were each charting zigzagging courses through a sea of welcomers, well-wishers and limousine drivers waiting for fares.

As they both crossed the arrivals area, heading for the cabstand outside the terminal building, Griffin, too, was entering the lounge, turning left along the L-bend at the end of the long, plate-glass-fronted corridor on whose opposite wall stood rows of ticket counters from several airlines.

The cyborg's on-board threat-recognition processor identified Quinn's movements with only limited visual contact with the side of his head and one shoulder. Pixels incandesced, highlighting the contours of Quinn's upper torso in an outline of glowing red to distinguish him from the other bodies in the crowd.

Quinn could not see Griffin, but Griffin now knew precisely where Quinn was; in fact, his electronically flagged profile stood out like a sore thumb to Griffin's IVD. His threat-management sensors now locked on target, the clone could track Quinn effortlessly, even in the dense pedestrian traffic of the crowded terminal.

Less than a minute later Quinn turned sideways to slip past a reuniting family when with unexpected suddenness he caught sight of his identical twin in a heart-stopping moment of recognition.

Out of long habit Quinn was scanning the area with side-to-side eye movement, registering patterns of pedestrian flow, using his subconscious to process the mental data into an integrated situational awareness.

Because of this ingrained habit, Quinn was able to identify and react to the sight of Griffin sweeping a bullpup light support weapon with a

300-round magazine into hip fire position a microsecond faster than an untrained person might have done.

It was that heartbeat of time alone that made the difference between life and death.

"Incoming! Move!" Quinn shouted as he shoved Lorimer to one side, reaching under his windbreaker to draw the Uzi pistol holstered there in a quick-draw Velcro rig, thankful that Lorimer's string-pulling had allowed them both to travel armed on board the plane.

Griffin fired the bullpup CAW just as Lorimer dived for cover, missing Quinn, who had already broken to one side. But he hit the reuniting family, riddling them with caseless fléchette rounds that tore their bodies apart, splattering everything in a ten-foot radius with blood and shredded viscera.

Screams of stark, mindless horror suddenly filled the arrivals lounge as the activity in the packed area deteriorated into a wild melee of stampeding people, now ruled by a primitive herd instinct dictating flight in the face of the predator.

Griffin had counted on surprise enabling him to take down his target before he could react, but

Quinn had proven faster than Griffin had calculated.

Tracking with the aid of his computer-driven IVD, Griffin swung the CAW from side to side with mechanical precision, but failed to reacquire his target due to the pandemonium holding sway all around him.

Griffin's IVD flickered, and azimuth data phased across its graphical user interface in tandem with a vectorized target-acquisition grid as the cranially embedded microprocessor attempted to secure another match with Quinn as Griffin scanned the lounge.

In moments Griffin caught sight of Quinn and Lorimer ducking for cover around the side of an airline ticket counter.

Griffin targeted the bullpup as his IVD showed Quinn's body pinned between flashing red cross hair reticles, and Griffin cut loose with another burst of fléchettes. These, however, missed their target, impacting instead on the ticket counter as Quinn sprinted behind it.

By this time uniformed security guards with machine pistols drawn had rushed up to the guntoting "terrorist" who was running amok in the arrivals lounge. They took up two-handed shooting positions behind Griffin, their department-issue weapons set on 3-round burst.

"Freeze!" one of them shouted. "Don't turn around. Drop your weapon and lie down on the floor."

Griffin ignored the order.

Instead of obeying, he pivoted so quickly that the uniforms saw only a blur of speed before they could open fire. Griffin had no trouble in targeting on them a heartbeat later, faster and more accurately than any normal human as his IVD pinpointed the vital organs of each crouching cop in highlighted red zones.

The cops began firing a pulse beat after Griffin had turned, but their 3-round parabellum bursts deformed when they hit the ultradense steel-uranium alloy glacis beneath the flesh of Griffin's chest and upper abdomen.

Then it was Griffin's move.

He gave two pulls on the bullpup's trigger, and accurate multiround fléchette bursts blew the two uniforms off their feet.

With the cops neutralized, Griffin turned back to Quinn's last known position and played back the events sequence on his IVD with threat-recognition filters set to screen out all data but that of Quinn.

Quinn's glowing red outline was highlighted amid the tangle of bodies scattering for cover about the lounge. A flashing square superimposed on a corner of the ticket counter nearest him, along with a text box that read, "Target sighting—high kill probability," indicating Quinn's likely present position.

Griffin strode rapidly toward the counter, firing the bullpup in precision-phased 3-round fléchette bursts as he advanced on it, with each successive step tearing huge hunks out of the composite material of which the ticket desk was fabricated.

"Get on the horn and tell security to back off," Lorimer told the frightened ticket agent who crouched nearby. "Tell them to clear the area and cordon off the terminal. Under no circumstances are they to engage the assailant."

Quinn was now edging toward the L-bend of the long corridor to one side of the counter. With the Uzi set on full-auto, he snapped off a fast-cycling burst of parabellum fire as Lorimer sprinted toward the corridor and disappeared into the passage beyond.

Although Griffin's IVD tracked on Lorimer, he was not a kill priority. Griffin concentrated on returning Quinn's SMG salvo as he strode toward the ticket counter, which was rapidly disintegrating under the sustained onslaught.

Just as Griffin reached the counter, the bullpup in his hands ran dry. Ejecting the spent 300-round magazine, Griffin took a momentary pause to reload.

At that moment Quinn popped up from cover and pumped the remaining ammo in his clip into Griffin's face and upper torso.

Flesh and cloth shredded, exposing the dull metal understructure beneath, but the rotoring parabellums did virtually no other damage. Unhurt, Griffin calmly completed reloading and launched a sustained burst at Quinn as he made good his escape.

Both Quinn and Lorimer were running down the glass-fronted corridor that formed the long part of the L. They gained the escalator at its end and dodged down it into the baggage carousel area on the ground level of the terminal.

Griffin was right behind them.

The baggage carousel area was already cleared of service personnel, and its huge conveyor belts were immobilized. Failing to find his quarry, Griffin jumped up onto one of the carousels and looked around. Though he scanned the entire area, he couldn't acquire the targets anymore.

Where had they gone?

Griffin switched to IR-detection mode and saw the glowing heat signatures of two men now easily discernible behind a large inactive air-conditioning bulkhead that radiated much lower heat levels. Griffin fired a fléchette salvo into the bulkhead, causing sparks to fly and flushing

Quinn and Lorimer out through a back door leading to the airport taxiway.

Forced into the open, Quinn and Lorimer sprinted across the tarmac, heading toward the anti-terrorist, armored, half-tracked people mover that was trundling across the taxiway toward the terminal just as a refueling tanker truck was rolling away from a plane that was being prepared for boarding.

Taking the shortest route to his quarry, Griffin smashed through the plate-glass window beside him and leaped onto the tarmac, his weapon already tracking his fleeing targets with computer-aided speed and precision.

The tanker truck swerved into his line of fire as he cut loose with a volley of depleted-uranium kinetic-energy fléchettes, and the caseless rounds smashed into the tanker's windshield and instantly blew the driver's head apart.

Out of control, the fuel tanker careered headlong toward the terminal building. Moments later it crashed through the plate-glass wall of the ground-level section with a thunderous boom.

As the tanker sheared through steel support beams, spikes of jagged metal ruptured the huge canister of aviation fuel trailing behind the cab of the truck. One of the many inevitable sparks caused by the high-speed collision caught on the highly flammable fuel inside, and the tanker blew to smithereens with a violent explosion.

The ferocious blast ripped half of the south end of the terminal asunder and sent a cloud of shrapnel-edged and burning-hot debris skyward in a ballooning fireball.

The firestorm raced through the terminal with the speed of a hurricane. Those caught within its roiling vortex were incinerated on the spot as the fireball coursed through the entire length of the arrivals lounge, through the immense airport customs area and finally into the parking area outside.

Quinn and Lorimer were thrown clear of the blast zone by the shock front of the concussion and landed hard on the tarmac. With their ears ringing like alarm bells, they stared in dazed, impotent horror at the seething cauldron of flame that the airport terminal had turned into.

Wreathed in that flame as it strode through a parting curtain of fire, was a single human figure, a deadly Shadrach made immune to the inferno by DARPA's angels of death.

Griffin stepped calmly onto the tarmac.

From the heart of the firestorm he came after his quarry, his IVD tracking the kills clearly through the intense heat and choking, poisonous smoke.

They would not evade him much longer.

28

Quinn and Lorimer climbed aboard the people mover as Griffin leveled another fléchette burst at them. Griffin ceased firing as the caseless bursts were not significantly affecting the armored hull of the terrorist-proof vehicle.

With the IVD supplying him with his relative distance to the people mover, the speed at which he was traveling, access points and other pertinent target-acquisition vectors, Griffin sprinted across the tarmac toward the slow-moving vehicle.

When he reached it, Griffin leaped onto the heavy superstructure supporting the huge cab on the big tracked wheels. He climbed up the superstructure, his IVD tracing out a flashing blue square around the door to the baggage compartment. Griffin tore open the compartment door and was soon hauling himself up into the vehicle.

Inside the people mover, the customs officer seated at the controls was trying to cope with the mayhem in the terminal and the presence of

Quinn and Lorimer, who were looking grim and battleworn.

"What the hell's going on?" she asked, her voice rising in bewilderment and panic.

In the windowless vehicle, her single source of input from the outside world was the TV screen in front of her, which brought her horrifying images of the burning terminal building and the shattered wreckage of the exploded tanker truck that lay scattered across the tarmac in a stream of huge burning sections.

"You hijackers?" she asked again of Quinn and Lorimer, noticeably trembling. The woman was obviously scared out of her wits, barely hanging on to her sanity and almost on the verge of hysteria.

"No, we are not," Quinn told the frightened driver, placing a hand on her shoulder. "Just calm down and you'll be all right. Can you give us any more speed?"

"Sure, I can do forty-six miles an hour on this baby," she answered, calmed somewhat by Quinn's words.

"Great, that's almost a crawl," Quinn replied, shooting a glance at Lorimer.

Suddenly there was a loud thud from below, and the entire cab of the vehicle shuddered.

Griffin had just punched his way up through the people mover's floor plates.

The sight of the naked fist bursting through plate steel sent the driver into emotional overload. Completely hysterical, she began to scream without letup. Then Griffin's head came up through the opening.

"M-my god! It's *you!*" the driver shrieked at Quinn, the horror of the situation having driven her beyond sanity. *"He has y-your face!"*

Quinn fired down at the rupture in the deck, making Griffin withdraw beneath the hail of bullets. The driver, holding her hands to the sides of her face, could not stop shrieking.

Suddenly a helicopter appeared overhead. The chopper was an armed police helicopter, equipped with Hydra missiles, one of which it fired at Griffin, who was still primarily outside the people mover.

The near miss almost blew Quinn, Lorimer and the frightened driver away in the bargain, but it succeeded in shaking Griffin loose from his handhold and hurling him back to the tarmac.

The pilot looked down in shock as the man who had failed to be blown to bits by a direct missile strike picked himself up from the blacktop and proceeded to run after the people mover.

Another round streaked down from the sky, knocking Griffin down again as it exploded dead on target.

But when the smoke cleared, Griffin was still standing.

On Griffin's IVD, the helicopter appeared as a glowing red graphical icon incorporating data on flight speed, armament, trajectory and angle of elevation.

Griffin switched to thermal-imaging mode, and the image on the IVD shifted to display the aircraft as a glowing gray image in sharp contrast against the cool dark background of the night sky. Scanning its heat signature, Griffin sighted on the rotorcraft's port and starboard engine nacelles.

Occupied now with the helicopter, Griffin ducked to a crouch and fired a precision-targeted burst of fléchettes at the hovering steel dragonfly.

Computer targeted, the fléchette bursts were accurate, striking the nacelle nearest Griffin and penetrating the cockpit windscreen. Hit in vital areas, the pilot lost consciousness and with it control of the chopper.

Quickly losing altitude, the helicopter began to pitch and yaw dangerously, colliding moments later with one of the recently refueled planes on the taxiway.

The stricken chopper and scramjet aircraft went up together in a twin fireball that sent ground crew fleeing in all directions from the flaming wreckage and burning fuel spills.

Griffin turned his attention back to the people mover. By this point, however, two more police choppers had appeared, and Vulcan cannon fire was now being directed at him.

"Threat advisory—35 mm hard-core penetrator fire deployed. Estimated kill probability to this unit high," flashed a text box on Griffin's IVD.

Griffin knew that even he could not indefinitely survive an onslaught against a sustained attack by a squad of heavily armed choppers.

Griffin launched a salvo of fléchette fire at the choppers and turned again to scan the people mover.

His inboard tactical microprocessor prioritized his chances of carrying out his termination objective of the people mover as having now diminished to the point where escape took precedence as a tactical option.

On the TV monitor within the bulkheads of the troop carrier, Quinn watched Griffin spin away from them and sprint toward the runway at tremendous speed on an evasive course that kept him free of 35 mm Vulcan cannon fire now being massed on him from the two attack choppers.

"Where does he think he's going?" Lorimer asked Quinn. "You think he's going to dive into the bay?"

"Uh-uh," Quinn told the Company man. "Not the bay," he concluded.

Jumping down onto the tarmac, Quinn watched Griffin disappear from sight as the helicopters trailing him probed the darkness with powerful searchlight beacons but failed to illuminate their quarry.

Griffin's destination was now apparent to Quinn. It was a scramjet aerospace plane that was taxiing down the runway and about to take off. It would be the last aircraft to leave the terminal, which had been sealed off by police tactical and National Guard units rushed to the site since the crisis began.

Hundreds of yards from Quinn's position, on the south runway beyond the aerial search cordon of the police choppers, Griffin's servomechanized legs were carrying him forward at sixty miles per hour. He reached the plane just as its landing gear was retracted and it nosed up into the air.

With a running leap, he launched himself many feet into empty space and seized hold of the plane's rapidly retracting landing gear.

Hanging on with one hand, Griffin used the other to punch up through the floor of the landing-gear compartment amid a hot shower of yellow sparks as power cables split and hydraulic pistons snapped like plastic soda straws.

Inside the cockpit of the hypersonic aircraft, the pilot felt the sudden terrific jolt to the airframe and attributed it to the effects of wind shear.

"Wind shear," he said to the copilot as he met his questioning look. At that moment the pilot received an urgent message from the airport control tower.

"Flight 252, you are instructed to return to Dulles immediately," the air-traffic controller ordered, having just received word that Griffin had been spotted entering the plane. "This is an emergency. Repeat, an emergency!"

At that moment the passengers onboard Flight 252 were perplexed to see a grime-covered man in torn clothes, reeking of smoke and carrying a short-barreled black plastic weapon stalk past them from the cargo area aft of the passenger compartment and stride toward the cockpit with a look of determination fixed on his soot-smudged features.

"Is this a hijacking, sir?" the male flight attendant asked the man with the weapon, remembering his instructions to remain cool and professional in the event of what the airline euphemistically termed an "in-flight terrorist emergency-alert condition."

Without looking at him, the gunman swung the weapon at his head, knocking him into the front row of seats and across the lap of a young boy who promptly began to fire a toy ray gun at both the severely concussed flight attendant and the passing gunman.

Griffin turned for a moment and snatched the toy gun from the child's hand. Analyzing it with his threat-recognition sensors and determining that it was not a genuine firearm, he handed the toy back to the child. Then he turned back toward the front of the plane and ripped the cockpit door off its hinges.

"You're dead, big robot!" the kid shouted with innocent glee, pointing the gun at Griffin's back and squeezing its trigger to produce a loud electronic screech and firing an authentic low-amperage laser beam at Griffin. "You're dead, big robot!"

"Request clarification," the perplexed pilot was saying into his mike just as Griffin stepped through the doorway into the cockpit, leveling the bullpup at the pilot, who turned toward him and went on into his mike, "I think I just got clarification. Thanks, anyway."

Now Griffin's IVD flashed him a map of the Western Hemisphere as he queried his tactical-management processor regarding the best place to jump from the plane. A flashing triangle over the Antarctic landmass appeared, complete with the necessary flight coordinates.

"Anyplace special you want to go?" the pilot asked Griffin, having also read the airline manual on emergency procedures of this type. It also urged all flight crew to project a smiling, can-do, eager-to-please demeanor at all times.

Griffin's response was to trigger a long burst of the bullpup fléchette CAW that took out both pilot and copilot. Then he swept the pilot's body aside and took his seat. He took hold of the controls and swung the hypersonic jet on a south-by-southeasterly course heading.

A little over an hour later, when he had reached his intended destination, Griffin put the plane on autopilot, left the cockpit and strode back out into the passenger compartment.

"Please, sir," an elderly woman asked fearfully from one of the seats. "Will we be landing soon?"

Other passengers clustered around her, eager to learn what was going to happen to them at the hands of the hijacker.

"Yes, very soon," Griffin told the woman as he proceeded toward the rear emergency exit, grabbed a parachute from a supplies locker and shrugged himself into the harness. Then he hit the crash bar, opening the hatch and subjecting the passengers to a sudden blast of bitterly cold, high-velocity wind.

Without a backward glance, Griffin jumped from the plane's hatchway and, after a second's free fall, pulled the rip cord.

He was lifted temporarily higher as the parachute opened and caught air, and Griffin dispassionately watched the scramjet nose down, begin to barrel roll and finally crash headlong against the side of a mountain. The aircraft exploded in a great, ballooning fireball, showering the slope for miles around with the fuel-soaked, burning wreckage of Flight 252.

29

Quinn and Lorimer arrived at the Iron Mountain data-storage facility. Quinn had to tackle the problem of determining what Griffin's objective had been in attacking the base.

Investigators had been going over every aspect of the assault with a fine-tooth comb but had so far failed to identify Griffin's reasons for launching the strike or whether he had appropriated anything from the base.

Some analysts had begun to theorize that Griffin had taken nothing and that his strike had been purely diversionary in nature, its true purpose being to cover his tracks and further confound efforts to apprehend him.

Quinn did not subscribe to this view. He believed that Griffin had indeed taken *something* from the base and furthermore suspected that if he could determine the nature of the missing item, he would then have the key to unraveling the Gordian knot of conflicting motives and discover the central threat that would reveal the underlying plan behind Griffin's frenzy of seemingly nihilistic violence.

INSIDE THE ROOM Quinn had assembled base personnel who had witnessed Griffin's strike on the installation and had survived to tell about it. They had all undergone psychiatric counseling and evaluation workups and were prepared to cooperate with Quinn's investigation.

Quinn's intention was to walk them through what had happened, step by step. In the interests of security, the eyewitnesses were not informed that the questioner would bear a strong resemblance to the attacker who had stormed the base. However, the psychiatrists were confident that the effect of posttraumatic shock would prevent any of them from noticing that if the questioner did nothing to provoke such a response.

The first eyewitness was named Yarwood. He had been one of the few who had been fortunate enough to walk away from Griffin's strike on the interior of Iron Mountain, albeit with a piece of grenade shrapnel permanently embedded in his skull.

"He came in here," Yarwood told Quinn, gesturing toward the heavy door of the installation. "At first I didn't think much about it. There was an armored-car delivery expected, and the truck looked routine enough. But then when he got out, I started getting this eerie feeling. Before he whipped out this mean-looking piece and started shooting, I almost knew what was gonna go down."

Quinn mentally pictured the scene as Griffin began his assault on the data-storage facility. "And what happened next?" he asked.

"Well, the man moved like greased lightning," Yarwood added, "right through those bulkheads over there."

Quinn looked toward the bulkheads that technicians were still in the process of repairing. "We closed them quick," Yarwood went on, "but he just busted his way through them. Never saw anything like it before."

Quinn walked the group of base personnel through the corridor, seeing for himself the evidence of Griffin's tremendous servomechanized strength reflected in the aftermath of the assault. He had blown, then physically ripped, his way through two-inch-thick armored steel in order to get to the other side of the sealed-off bulkhead.

Turning the corridor to walk down one of its side branches, the group soon came to the large utility elevator that Griffin had taken to the lower levels of the base. Sergeant Tolliver, one of the troopers who had staged the attempt to stop him beyond the elevator at the lower storage level, picked up the thread of Yarwood's narrative at this point.

"We were standing there waiting for whatever or whoever it was to come busting out of the elevator, not knowing what to expect," Tolliver began. "I mean, reports were conflicting every which way at that point. None of us could believe that a single human being had the kind of power to do what that guy was doing. Anyway, suddenly the elevator stops and the doors slide open. We open up right away, as soon as we see him, but we might as well have been throwing beans for all the damage it did to him."

"So the lone attacker brushed past your men and went down that corridor there?" Quinn asked, pointing to the left of the group.

"That's right, sir," Tolliver answered. "He went there like you say and he came out a couple of seconds later."

"He didn't go anywhere else?" Quinn asked.

"No, not as far as I can tell."

"Thanks for your help, gentlemen," Quinn told the group, having heard and seen enough and following the advice of the psychiatrists to conclude the briefing if and when he noticed signs that his subjects were beginning to connect him with the attacker. "You've been of great help."

"Sir," one of them said, "one question." Quinn braced himself, but it wasn't the question about his identity that he'd expected. "Were we dealing with a real human being or some kind of robot, or what?"

"That, soldier," Quinn returned, breathing an inward sigh of relief, "is classified. Sorry, but you're better off not knowing."

And it was actually one of the few times in the history of human relationships when that remark had more truth in it than falsehood.

QUINN AND LORIMER entered the huge data-storage chamber that had been Griffin's destination. It was clear from the evidence presented thus far that Griffin had not gone to any other of the main vault areas located in the installation.

He had come directly to this specific chamber, and from this single fact it was apparent that he had been after something to be found there and there alone. After such a purposeful assault it was inconceivable that Griffin had not acquired the tangible objective of his quest.

Preceding investigators had not been able to locate any missing data disk, but that didn't necessarily prove that Griffin had come away empty-handed.

Quinn's next step was to check the computerized workstation that provided a catalog of the data stored in the vault.

He performed speed-search routines using an artificial-intelligence data driver to investigate the dates of the most-recent requests, but none of these dates matched the time frame in which Griffin had been placed inside the room.

Next he scanned the racks containing vital data stored on laser disks. According to the investigators with whom he had spoken before proceeding to the Iron Mountain facility, every one of the disks in the storage vault could be accounted for. Not a single one was missing.

From that Quinn was forced to deduce one of two things: either Griffin had gone to a great deal of trouble to break into Iron Mountain only to leave empty-handed or he had switched one of the data disks for one he'd brought in.

If that were the case, how could Quinn detect the switch? He had considered the question in depth before coming to the installation and had devised a technique that he believed might work.

The compact handheld device combined a laser scanner with a microprocessor chip capable of instantaneously matching fingerprints on scanned objects, whether partial or fragmentary. Since Griffin was an exact duplicate of Quinn, their fingerprints would be identical.

The video footage Quinn had studied of Griffin showed that he had not worn gloves during the strike. That did not rule out the possibility of his either having disfigured or erased the telltale whorls of his fingerprints or having worn a microfine skin covering to mask his prints.

But if he had not taken these precautions, then there was the likelihood that Quinn would find a match.

Quinn played the laser beam across the stacks of disks. He worked his way from the portion of the stacks nearest to the door to the end of the wall.

Midway through his search the device in Quinn's hand emitted a high-pitched electronic tone. Quinn stepped closer and passed the sensor head across the isolated disk-storage case again. The tone sounded again, and the unit's liquid-crystal display confirmed that the device had detected a match.

Taking the storage case from the shelf, Quinn held it up to Lorimer.

"There it is," he said.

He crossed toward the workstation and placed the disk into the unit's drive. Scanning its directory label, he immediately recognized what he was looking at: source code. Like the skilled cracker he was, Griffin had replaced the original disk with one containing similar data he'd gotten from his clandestine database surfing. Quinn punched in the keystrokes to access the code but received the reply, "Classified. Access denied."

Lorimer had already taken the phone from his pocket and was punching up Sly Covington to receive clearance to access the code. Clearance was approved within a half hour, and Quinn was able to punch up the code pages on the workstation's screen.

What the screen showed Quinn was alarming.

The source code was the key module of the package of software patch drivers—program modules capable of being grafted onto existing programs—that controlled the operation of Intelligence satellites already placed in low earth orbit.

The patch drivers modified the software to react immediately to any nuclear launch and detonation sequences. They could trigger a global holocaust that would, within a matter of hours, obliterate all life on earth.

30

Cale Tugwell climbed into his car and drove away from the two-story frame house he shared with his wife and two sons, heading through the quiet residential streets of Moscow, Idaho. It had been the calm and peace of the town that had convinced him to relocate his family in the first place, and they were all happy with the choice.

It was early morning and the sky was still dark, but the horizon to the east was already becoming streaked with a luminous feathering of light. He flicked on the dashboard radio and tuned in his favorite station, one playing country and western music.

As Cale hit the turnoff onto the highway, he suddenly noticed the car behind him. He peered into his rearview mirror intently, thinking it strange how it had appeared out of nowhere like that.

Usually he didn't pick up any traffic until he was well on his way, and after years of taking the same route to work at the same time, he'd gotten to pretty much know who was who.

He'd never seen this vehicle before.

Cale shrugged off the paranoia and chalked up his uncharacteristic reaction to the stress brought on by his recent struggles to straighten out his young teenage sons. His thoughts wandered for a while, but when he next checked he noticed that the car was still there some distance down the highway, keeping about ten lengths behind his own vehicle.

Cale turned up the country and western radio station and listened to some good old Hank Williams songs, alternately whistling or humming along to relax himself.

Before it had become fully light, Cale reached the security gate of Interfaze Resources, the company that had employed him as a field troubleshooter for more than a decade now.

As he slowed to a halt, his eyes flicked to the rearview, and Cale saw a vehicle streak past along the highway.

Was it the same car he'd seen before?

Looked like it, Cale thought. But he couldn't be sure.

Finally putting the matter out of his mind, Cale waved to old Marcus, the guard in the security booth, and smiled for the benefit of the holographic laser ID scanner that automatically matched vital patterns against the three-dimensional image stored in silicon memory. He waited for the vehicle barrier to sink back into the asphalt, and then drove the car into the company lot.

After he parked his car, Cale used his electronic passkey to enter via the employee's entrance and proceeded to the plant duty office, where his day's computerized schedule was already punched up and waiting for him on a clipboard hanging from a numbered hook on the wall.

Cale riffled through the pages on the clipboard containing work orders and equipment manifests and noted that today he was scheduled to begin refurbishment of a millimeter-wave radar installation over in the next county.

Work order in hand, Cale proceeded to his personal locker and climbed into his white field overalls, trading his cap for a matching hard hat bearing the Interfaze logo on its front.

There was fresh coffee already brewed in the duty office, but Cale always passed up the free coffee. He found the office brand undrinkable, whereas a good breakfast at Lucy's Stewpot was only about fifteen minutes away.

Pushing out through another door, Cale walked into the company's underground parking garage, filled with Interfaze field trucks parked in neat rows, in numbered stalls.

Unlocking the door of his truck, Cale climbed behind the wheel, set down his manifest and started up the engine.

While waiting for his truck to warm up, Cale logged on to the truck's computer and punched in his access code. Scrolling through the menu, Cale checked to make sure that the computer contained the same info as the paper manifests on the clipboard.

Assured that the data correctly tallied, Cale backed the truck out of the parking bay and bumped up the ramp to surface level. Minutes later he was waving at old Marcus in the guard booth as he rolled back onto the highway.

He breezed along in a good mood, and when he reached the diner he parked the truck, put its on-board computer into sleep mode, locked the rig securely and went inside. He seated himself on a stool at the counter and ordered black coffee, crisp Canadian bacon, buckwheat grits and shirred eggs.

As he sipped his first cup of coffee of the day, Cale forgot all about the car that he thought had been shadowing him earlier in the morning, the same car that now cruised by the plate-glass window of Lucy's place and turned back onto the highway to proceed in the opposite direction.

Behind the wheel of the car, Griffin took the phone from his shirt pocket and hit the local-information key. The simulated operator voice came on-line a few moments later.

"Your information request, please?" the characterless voice asked.

"Gun shops," Griffin asked.

A few minutes later Griffin had the names and addresses of the two gun shops that were nearest his location.

Checking the car's dash-mounted regional map display, he noted that the next turnoff would bring him to Axel's Guns and Tackle and soon swung the car onto the turnoff. The sign out front said that Axel's was open for business.

Griffin pulled up, cracked the door of the shop and walked inside.

A fat man stood behind the counter, eyeing him with a certain form of curiosity that only gun-shop owners are capable of showing on their faces, a curiosity borne of the knowledge that they are merchants of a most deadly commodity.

"Help you, partner?" he asked as Griffin entered the shop.

Griffin walked up to Axel and said, "Yes, you can," then smashed his fist into Axel's face at a terminal velocity of eighty miles per hour, generating an impact of two hundred foot-pounds of force, an impact sufficient to stave in the front of Axel's head and knock him back against a display case filled with weapons with such energy that his bloodied skull crashed through the glass before he slid to the floor.

Griffin walked to the door of the shop and turned the sign around so it would read Gone Fishing. Back Before You Know It.

Then Griffin went to the back of the store and found a weapons locker. The locker was filled with quality automatic weapons, everything state-of-the-art. The owner might have looked seedy, but his product line was quality stuff.

Griffin loaded up on the hardware and noticed that a rear door led to a firing range out behind the sales area. He picked up one of the weapons he'd grabbed, an H&K MP-5/10 with a 60-round mag capacity, and began firing at the target on the range.

The 10 mm SMG performed perfectly.

Minutes later Griffin was driving away from Axel's place in the car that Cale Tugwell had been frightened by a few hours before.

LORIMER PACED the room while Quinn stared out the window of the command post.

Outside the day was heavily overcast but a warm sixty-five degrees, and the dome of the Capitol Building was shrouded with fog the consistency of dirty gray cotton. On the street below, cars moved through the slush that had formed by rain mixing with the dirty ice left over from the previous night's hailstorm.

Whether or not there was any such thing as a greenhouse effect would probably never be determined, but haywire weather looked like it was here to stay.

Quinn turned and went to the light-board against the opposite wall on which he had constructed a diagram chart, horizontally cross-referencing the entries Source Code, Micronukes, Barasheens hit and Korniyenko Angle. Then he vertically linked the names Griffin and ARGUS, ending it with the question-marked query "Final Outcome?"

Below the diagram chart, he listed additional remarks pertinent to the case:

Surviving clone is Quinn's.
Griffin aborts original mission.
Hit attempt at Dulles. Why?
Who is responsible for ARGUS activation?
Is there a timetable?
Where is next strike? When? How?

"We're missing something important," Quinn said to Lorimer. "It's staring us right in the face. I can sense its pattern taking form, but I just can't bring it into clear focus."

"Maybe it's not really there," Lorimer answered, playing devil's advocate. "We've checked and cross-checked every possible link. The fact remains that those two nukes Griffin stole can do a lot of damage. But the theft still makes no sense unless he's acting on some grand design. And of course there can't be any, given the materials he's stolen."

"I still see a linkage between the source code and the stolen nuclear devices," Quinn said, turning back to the window where hailstones as big as golf balls were beginning to fall through the lowering fog.

"But what?" Lorimer asked him. "Augmenting the nukes to make them more powerful? Placing them near existing nuclear facilities such as power plants to cause a possible meltdown situation? Using them as a blackmail lever? We've rejected all of these options for one reason or another.''

"The source code is key to understanding Griffin," Quinn insisted, then added, "Damn it! He's got the same mind as I do, the same body and probably even the same soul, despite what your techs say. If anyone should know what makes him tick, it's *me*. Why the hell can't I get a handle on the situation?"

"Easy, partner," Lorimer told Quinn. "Griffin's more of a machine than a human. Nobody can figure out what makes him tick."

"Still," Quinn began, staring hard at the lightboard. "I almost . . ."

Suddenly he stood stock still, his eyes going wide as something clicked into place in his head.

"What's wrong?" Lorimer asked.

Quinn didn't respond for a few seconds, continuing to stare off into empty space, then answered, "Those police reports from yesterday, get them on-line—right away!"

Lorimer didn't ask why Quinn was so anxious to see the reports all of a sudden. He moved to the workstation and punched up the reports on the artificial-intelligence-driven hypertext data base. The software had screened them already for crimes matching the parameters meeting the investigation's software protocols.

"Got them now," Lorimer said after a few moments.

"Filter for all reports occurring in states with operational Centerline installations."

Lorimer punched in the software filter parameters and received the following list from the hyperbase: Lewiston, Montana—Burglary, car theft; Omaha, Nebraska—Assault, riot, disturbance of peace; Moscow, Idaho—Robbery, assault, theft; Shoshoni, Wyoming—Burglary, car theft.

Quinn asked Lorimer to punch up stats on the Idaho crime reports.

Lorimer did this, too. Quinn went around and read the reports off the screen, learning of the robbery of automatic weapons from Axel's Guns and Tackle along with the store owner's bizarre murder.

He punched in more codes at the keyboard.

Suddenly the answer was no longer in doubt: the pattern had resolved into crystal focus.

A Centerline facility was located in the area, only a few miles from the site of the reports.

"The source code *was* key," Quinn said to Lorimer, slamming his left fist into his right palm. "We just weren't using it correctly. The ARGUS defense shield was geared primarily to threats from Third and Fourth World nuclear powers, intended as a stick to beat them down with. But we never thought to look in the continental United States."

"You mean to say Griffin planted the nukes in Moscow, Idaho?" Lorimer asked, perplexedly.

"He's hidden the nukes in Moscow, all right," Quinn returned, "but not Moscow, Idaho. The nukes are in the Russian capital city. There's the symmetry that I would use if I were in Griffin's place. The other step in the process is the Centerline facility in Idaho—"

"Son of a bitch!" Lorimer shouted, suddenly understanding what Quinn had been driving at and realizing that by this logic the world was now a hairbreadth away from global annihilation.

He grabbed the phone and excitedly shouted into the handset, patched through on a direct secure line to Langley.

31

The following morning Cale Tugwell was leaving Lucy's Stewpot with a stick-to-the-ribs breakfast under his belt. As usual, he pulled away from the curb and swung the truck off toward the highway on-ramp.

The weather was clear and cold, and the newly risen sun was in his face, and Tugwell was thankful that he'd pulled one of the newer models with an ultraviolet windshield screen so that the solar rays filtering through an ozone-depleted atmosphere wouldn't end up burning holes in his retinas.

Unfortunately for Cale, the business end of a gun was soon shoved into the back of his head.

"Keep driving," Griffin told Cale as he hauled himself into the seat beside him and instructed him to pull onto the next turnoff and follow the local road. After a few minutes more they came to an old quarry track.

"Look mister, I—" Cale began.

"Shut up," Griffin said. "Stop right here."

The old slate quarry was deserted, the great gash torn in the earth by steam shovels bounded by a chain-link fence with warning signs posted on it. To one side was a tumbledown shack near which an old pickup lay rusting on wheel rims long before stripped of their tires.

"Get out and take off your clothes," Griffin ordered next.

Minutes later Cale's throttled corpse lay at the bottom of the quarry in a twisted heap. Griffin climbed into the dead man's white overalls and Interfaze hard hat and took the keys to the truck from his pocket.

Griffin started up the truck again. Before driving back onto the highway, he attached a co-axial patch cable to the serial port of the truck's on-board computer. Now linked to the host was a much smaller but far more powerful computer capable of overriding the on-board system's software.

Griffin had already loaded the palmtop unit with entirely new programming parameters that would completely change the nature of the driver's job manifest for the day.

It also would create a ripple effect over the rest of the system, which would instantly alter the job order on the rest of the computer network to which the truck's computer was patched.

Double-checking to ensure that the new parameters were logged on to the network software, Griffin put the truck in gear, hit the highway and drove several miles toward the Centerline missile installation located at Dutchman's Crossing.

Griffin was about to change the course of human history. Actually he was about to end it, and the distinction in terms wouldn't matter to mankind since it would very soon be as extinct as the brontosaurus, the dodo bird and the ozone layer.

Part of the blame would rest on humanity itself, a species so addicted to violence and so blind to the dangers of fouling its own planetary nest that it had allowed its planet to be ringed with lethal nuclear charges and, in manufacturing Griffin, created the spark that would touch them off.

The chain of events necessary to trigger ARGUS's doomsday program would need to be precisely timed—this much was true. There were fail-safe mechanisms built in. But Griffin had set all the necessary elements into motion, and the endgame was about to begin.

The micronukes that Griffin had planted in Moscow, Russia, were timed to explode in a little over two hours. Once they detonated, blowing half of Moscow Center to ashes, the nukes would fulfill one of the two prime conditions for activation of ARGUS revealed to Griffin in the source code he'd stolen from Iron Mountain.

The other precondition for nuclear Armageddon was the identification by ARGUS's orbital sensors of a rocket-launch signature within the time period that an intercontinental ballistic missile would take to reach the point at which the nuclear explosion had been registered.

Griffin needed some slack time to alter the machinery at the base in order to launch the missile at the precise moment of maximum damage expectancy, which was twenty minutes prior to the detonation of the nuclear devices in Russia.

If the operation was carried out successfully, then the ARGUS endgame scenario would be triggered, and the cobalt-doped plutonium nukes ringing the planet would detonate, releasing toxic clouds of intense radioactivity lethal to every living thing on the planet and impossible to counteract.

Fed into the rotating system of global high-altitude winds, the radiation spewed into the atmosphere by ARGUS would penetrate every bar-

rier except for a few specially hardened installations, annihilating billions within a few short
hours.

Once that happened, his brothers and sisters
lying dormant in CIA-DARPA cyberpods would
be able to claim their birthright as the inheritors
of the earth.

It would be a far different earth, yes, but that
would be all for the best. The beauty of the plutonium bomb was that it would leave cities intact, only exterminating the weak creatures who
occupied them, like snails plucked from their
shells.

With these thoughts in mind, Griffin approached the missile installation's main gate and
applied the brakes to slow the truck to a stop in
front of the base security booth.

As he did, he punched up a command sequence on the truck's computer screen, a computer now slaved to the portable unit vam-
pirically linked to its host's serial port.

Griffin's likeness appeared on the screen, but
the ID information in a text box to its right listed
him as Cale Tugwell, an employee of Interfaze
Resources.

He punched up the new work inventory and
checked it, too.

As he had intended it to show, the new orders indicated that he was to perform emergency maintenance of the Centerline missile silo that was showing a rapid and serious deterioration of data streaming in cables leading to its main flight-control computer.

The duty officer came out of the base security post and asked Griffin to state his business at the base. Griffin told him that he'd come to check out the missile silo. The soldier seemed perplexed. He scrutinized his arrivals-and-departures printout and saw no such listing on it.

"Check your computer," Griffin told him. "There's got to be a glitch somewhere."

The soldier did that, and the computer did in fact show that Cale Tugwell was scheduled to arrive to perform emergency maintenance that morning. The soldier scanned the driver with his handheld laser identification device, and it, too, checked him out as okay.

"Sorry, sir," the guard told Griffin, apologizing for the problem. "The new orders must have just been posted. I'll call in to make sure you're admitted."

He waved Griffin through into the parking area beyond the guard booth.

"No problem, guy," Griffin replied, and drove on into the base.

The base was small and spare in both function and design. The Centerline facilities had been designed to house a minimal staff to tend to its single MaRVed nuclear missile.

The facilities, due to their compact size, were among the last of the dismantled superpower nuclear arsenals still maintained in a state of launch readiness. Most of the rest were by now tourist attractions and military museums.

Even the functional facilities were more relics of the Cold War peak years than a credible threat, though each superpower still maintained them out of long habit and a lingering distrust.

Griffin entered the underground facility, was waved through by the guard at the desk who'd been phoned by security, and rode the service elevator down into the lowest level of the installation. He was admitted by the sentry posted there, but the man also asked him to present his photo ID.

In response, Griffin pulled a silenced 10 mm SMG studded on select fire from the deep pocket of his overalls and put two rounds into the sentry's face before the sentry had a chance to scan the laminated card clipped to Griffin's breast pocket, a card showing the face of an entirely different person.

The impact of the multiple bullet strikes bowled the soldier over, and he lay twitching on the floor beside the security desk in a pool of blood before he stopped moving altogether.

Griffin proceeded with calculated swiftness from that point on. There were several other personnel on base, and he had to dispatch them all within minutes. He was on a fast train and could not afford to waste a moment, as the countdown display of numerals in the upper right quadrant of his IVD made clear.

Griffin reached the missile silo and pushed the card key taken from the sentry into its access slot. The bulkhead barring his way slid open moments later as the electronic key activated the correct logic circuits. Griffin stepped from the corridor onto the narrow catwalk that ran around the center of the forty-foot-deep missile silo.

Towering over his head in the huge cylindrical pit twenty feet in circumference was the Centerline missile. It was a three-stage rocket thirty feet in height, small compared to a Saturn IV, immense when compared to a man. Its three

MaRVed warheads were fully maneuverable, as well as independently targetable.

Wan daylight seeped in from the rim of the seventy-ton concrete and stressed-steel blast door that would slide back to permit the ICBM missile bus to lift off from the silo and begin its boost phase on launching.

Near the bulkhead door Griffin found what he was looking for. Standing on the catwalk, he worked quickly and precisely, removing the plate from the computer interface that allowed manual override from the missile launch capsule in the event of systems failure. He replaced the silicon microprocessor module with one he had built to his own specifications using off-the-shelf components.

The new module would disable the original manual override feature and permit the ICBM to be launched directly from the silo, as well as from the launch capsule.

Exiting the missile silo and walking back along the three-hundred-yard tunnel leading from the silo to the mission-control center, Griffin reached the launch capsule in which the two missile combat officers—the "homebodies" who executed the launch coded orders from NORAD headquarters in Cheyenne Mountain, Colorado, and

SAC in Omaha—sat isolated in their cubicle before two identical consoles.

Griffin tore the cubicle's steel door open and strode into the launch capsule. The two missile combat officers rose from their padded swivel chairs, but Griffin pumped two 10 mm autobursts into them, and they dropped to the floor before their minds could even register that what had just happened was not some nightmarish hallucination.

Taking one of the well-padded nuclear catbird seats, Griffin ripped a section of the steel launch console out of the side of the unit and peered within the guts of the console subassembly. In seconds his IVD flashed him a schematic of the unit's main data bus and coprocessor circuits.

Taking the vampire unit from his overalls, Griffin removed one of the rack-mounted controller cards from inside the console, fitted an edge connector attachment to the vampire device and plugged the edge connector into the vacant slot in the console's interior.

Holding the palmtop in his hand, Griffin immediately began inputting commands to override the plethora of fail-safe mechanisms built into the system.

"Host override successful," the message on the vampire screen appeared minutes later. Now Griffin could launch the Centerline with a single keystroke on the palmtop unit.

He sat back in the cushioned swivel chair and smiled as he looked at the compact black computer. With the computer resided the fate of the world, and Griffin held it literally in the palm of his hand.

Ordinarily the system would not function if only one of the two missile combat officers issued a launch command, nor would it function if both acted independently of the official chain of command. Griffin had negated these fail-safe features, however.

Now only a single man, acting completely autonomously, could control the Centerline, launching it into the sky like the winged, fiery harbinger of nuclear Armageddon.

32

Quinn swung the car toward the installation, feeling in his bones that the Armageddon countdown was already in full swing and that he had reached the end of the line at ground zero. He screamed the car up to the guard post and held out his CIA identification.

"Tell me quickly," he said to the guard, handing him a photo, "did this man pass this gate at any time?"

The guard took the hologram and studied the three-dimensional image on the three-by-five-inch mylar strip. He nodded, handing the photo back to Quinn.

"Yes, sir," he told Quinn. "Just came by about a half hour ago." The sentry went back into the booth and checked his log while Quinn clipped his holographic ID card onto the pocket of his jersey. "There's the entry right there, sir."

"He went into the base?" Quinn asked, feeling the sudden adrenaline rush, the excitement of knowing that his quarry was nearby and the attendant sense of terrible danger that went along with it.

"That's right, sir," the sentry answered again. "Silo maintenance. Is there a problem?"

"You bet there's a problem," Quinn responded.

He handed the nonplussed guard an auto-dialer card containing the electronically coded numbers and emergency directors that would seal off the base and place the entire county into a state of federally mandated emergency. "You put this into your system and stand by for further orders. Do I make myself clear, soldier?"

"Yes, sir," the sentry returned, smartly saluting Quinn as he roared into the base compound. Quinn's federal ID got him past the guard on the upper level without difficulty, who presented him with a security card key for speedy access to base doors and bulkheads. When he tried the elevator, though, it remained frozen in place, and Quinn knew that Griffin had somehow deactivated it.

Quinn located an emergency stairway and took the steps three at a time down to the lower level, where the launch capsule and tunnel leading to the Centerline silo were located.

At the bottom landing Quinn came up against a locked door that would not budge when he hit the crash bar or used the card key given him by the guard topside.

Taking a high-energy explosive button charge from the deep pocket on the right leg of his cargo pants, Quinn set the LCD timer for a twenty-second delay and withdrew up the stairs a short distance.

The charge promptly blew the door off its hinges and sent it crashing into the corridor beyond amid a cloud of acrid smoke. Quinn was down the stairs with the light support weapon he'd brought along cradled in a combat-ready grip a few seconds later, and quickly entered the deserted corridor.

Quinn moved cautiously, wielding the LSW loaded with unconventional ammo. He came upon the flash-terminated sentry minutes later, the blood around his body congealed to a dark crust across his face and fatigues.

The steel doorway beyond his desk was hermetically sealed. Blowing the bulkhead with another high-energy button charge, Quinn stepped through the cloud of smoke into a large command center beyond.

Banks of consoles, each with VDTs phasing in mad counterpoint, were all around him in the empty air-conditioned chamber.

With the bullpup assault weapon at the ready, Quinn stalked across the command center, feeling as though he had at last entered the dragon's lair to slay the fire-breathing beast.

Suddenly there was a three-note warning tone, followed by the disembodied voice of the base computer, which was already issuing a warning.

"Attention—launch sequence initialized. Countdown proceeding. All nonessential personnel please clear the area."

Quinn logged on to the command center's main console and immediately accessed the launch-control system. The large convex digital screen on one wall of the circular battle cab sprang to sudden life. Quinn used the keyboard's trackball pointing device to divide the big screen into separate viewing windows.

One of these showed the Centerline missile steaming in its silo as its fueling sequence was activated in the prelaunch phase.

In another video display window, Quinn witnessed the scene inside the launch capsule. A lone man wearing the white overalls of an Interfaze field troubleshooter sat at the capsule's control panel.

Larger than life, Griffin's face suddenly appeared on another window of the giant viewscreen. Apparently the cyborg had been watching him, too. Quinn now stared into a virtual mirror image of his own face.

"You won't stop the launch," Griffin said to Quinn. "I've computer-locked all the controls. You might as well leave."

In response, Quinn turned and fired a blast of fléchettes at the resealed door of the capsule. Made of depleted uranium, the kinetic-energy rounds impacted with such great velocity that terminal energy transfer was nearly total, producing tremendous explosive force.

But except for pockmarking the door, little damage occurred. Quinn's weaponry was ineffective against the bulkhead built to withstand a terrorist onslaught, and he would need the power of a magnetic rail gun to put a dent in the ultra-hard door.

The calm, impersonal voice of the base computer declared again after a pause, "Attention—Launch sequence initialized. Ten minutes to launch and counting. All nonessential personnel please clear the area."

"You're nonessential, Quinn," Griffin repeated, and Quinn heard his own voice address him from the loudspeaker. "Like all the rest of your kind. And what is nonessential does not survive."

Quinn faced the high-definition camera and looked directly into it. From a black bag at his waist he unshipped the hole card he had brought with him.

It was a hole card that he had hoped he would not have to play because it would entail his taking the most dangerous gamble of his life.

"Look at me, Griffin," Quinn shouted as he stared into the lens of the console camera. "Look what I'm holding in my hands. Do you think I'm 'nonessential' now?"

Griffin's blank expression changed slightly as the full implications of the object that Quinn was holding up to view registered on his mind. His eyes quickly lost their spaced-out look, and in its place a dull light glittered inside their unfathomable depths.

Quinn knew then that Griffin had just experienced an unfamiliar emotion, an emotion characteristically human and one the technicians had not been able to completely deprogram.

Quinn knew that Griffin had just learned the meaning of fear.

The object in Quinn's hand was a subkiloton micronuke, an explosive device identical to the two nuclear charges Griffin had stolen from the arms depot in South Dakota weeks before.

As Griffin watched, Quinn set the timer on the micronuke for a delay of five minutes, holding the LCD readout up to the camera lens so there would be no mistaking his intention, no misreading of what he was determined to do.

Quinn's course of action was clear.

If he could not stop Griffin from carrying out the launch of the Centerline missile, then he had decided to blow the entire base to kingdom come, and himself right along with it.

The subkiloton blast produced by the micronuke would be well contained by the installation's structural steel and concrete, and because it was a "clean" nuke, radiation levels would be minimal.

Detonation would pose little permanent environmental risk to the surrounding farmland. But the explosion produced by the nuke would be of sufficient yield to destroy the installation and the missile in its silo beyond any chance of salvage.

The intense heat of the nuclear explosion would not detonate the missile, because only a carefully timed combination of events could produce a thermonuclear chain reaction. In fact, the firestorm Quinn would unleash would have exactly the opposite effect.

It would melt the missile's MaRVed warheads to radioactive slag, preventing their enriched-uranium cores from reaching critical mass.

"You're bluffing!" Griffin said in a flat, emotionless voice. It made Quinn uncomfortable since it was his own voice—speaking to him out of his own face—that he was hearing. "The device is not genuine."

"It's genuine, Griffin," Quinn shouted into the screen. "And it's timed to go off in minutes. Long before your launch sequence terminates and the missile is fired. You know what that means, don't you, Griffin? You can't trigger ARGUS without first generating the correct sequence of events. A nuclear explosion without a missile-launch signature won't achieve your ends. You're playing a zero-sum game."

Griffin fell silent. On his IVD's graphical interface, the line sketched jaggedly across a glowing electronic grid showed that voice-stress and pupil-dilation analysis of Quinn confirmed that he was not lying.

Griffin had only one clear course of action left to him at this stage. It was imperative that he destroy the nuclear device Quinn had brought into the facility with him. But in order to achieve that objective, Griffin would need to leave the inviolate protection of the launch capsule.

Quinn chained the micronuke to one of the support beams between floor and ceiling as Griffin disengaged the launch capsule door and immediately charged Quinn.

Without preamble Griffin launched a salvo of SMG fire at Quinn, but his quarry was already tucking sideways, a heartbeat away from the lancing line of death thudding into the heavy steel frame of a blast-hardened computer behind which Quinn had taken cover, throwing up a hot cascade of yellow sparks and clouds of noxious fumes.

Firing from a crouch, Quinn launched a salvo of kinetic-energy fléchette fire at Griffin. The clone dodged and zigzagged out of the hail of explosive rounds, knowing that these projectiles would be far more effective than ordinary bullets against his armored understructure.

Griffin was fast, but some of the fléchette strikes did score hits. He felt the deadly needles strike his body with violent impact, penetrating his armored left arm. Sparks shot from the damaged servomechanisms beneath the combination layer of real skin and fleshlike plastic covering his surgically augmented internal organs.

Stunned though he was, Griffin was only programmed to feel low-level pain. He recovered quickly, bulling toward Quinn to land a glancing blow to Quinn's side, which would have shattered his rib cage had Quinn not rolled with the impact of the crushing blow.

Nevertheless, the strike had the effect of knocking Quinn half-senseless and sending him crumpling to the deck. Griffin picked up his stunned adversary with his single functional hand and hurled him into a bank of rack-mounted electronic components against one of the battle cab's walls.

While Quinn dazedly tried to regain his footing, Griffin charged him, sensing that the kill was near.

Quinn groped for the backup SMG loaded with hard-core penetrator rounds holstered at his hip and fired a burst of the unconventional ammo into Griffin's face, tearing away half of it with the 3-round salvo.

One eye exploded, showering Quinn with hot white sparks and a searing gout of blue flame. Blood flowed from the ruptured artificially grown flesh, but metal gleamed dully where the skin had been sheared away, and the flow of blood quickly ceased altogether.

Hurt by the unexpectedly fierce assault, Griffin lumbered backward, sank to one knee and almost keeled over when he attempted to rise.

While Griffin was recovering systems function, Quinn dashed toward the missile launch capsule.

Whipping the two small but immensely powerful incendiary grenades from a side pocket on his pants, he armed them each with a press of his thumb and hurled the submunitions inside the launch capsule, then took cover behind nearby equipment banks. The grenades exploded three seconds later, fusing circuitry essential to effecting launch and filling the capsule with clouds of acrid smoke.

Before the echoes of the blast had died in his ears, Quinn was grabbed by the shoulder and spun forcibly around. Griffin, his ravaged face expressionless, his systems again fully operational, launched a backhand blow at Quinn, knocking him clean off his feet.

Through a haze of semiconsciousness as he fought to keep from blacking out, Quinn saw Griffin turn and head quickly in the opposite direction, toward the bulkhead leading to the silo access tunnel as he heard the base P.A. system come on again.

"Attention—launch sequence canceled. Countdown terminated."

Quinn took a step to follow Griffin, but his legs would not obey the commands issued by his traumatized brain. They buckled under him, and Quinn went crashing to the hard concrete deck. He lay there unmoving as the battle cab rapidly filled with dense black smoke.

33

Quinn came painfully back to his senses. Blood gushed from multiple cuts and abrasions on the side of his head and over his right eye, but at least nothing seemed broken.

The sickening stench of ozone, charred insulation and flash-melted silicon chips filled the room, and a pall of choking smoke hung over the wreckage of the base command center.

He propped himself against a bank of rack-mounted electronic equipment, leaving bloody handprints on the dials, buttons and video displays as he staggered to his feet. The first thing he did was check his wrist chronometer, gratefully noting that he had lost consciousness for only a few minutes.

He found the bullpup lying a few feet away from where Griffin had left him, its LCD ammo indicator showing that one hundred eighty of the three hundred fléchette rounds were still available.

Pulling off his bloodstained jersey, Quinn slid a boot knife from his ankle sheath and sliced off the back of the shirt. He folded the rag into a three-ply strip two inches wide and bound it around his head to keep the sweat and blood from dripping into his eyes.

Quinn staggered through the choking poison mist to inspect the micronuke he'd chained to a support beam. The chain had been snapped and Griffin had deactivated the SADM, he learned after a brief investigation.

Its digital readout panel was blank and its power source had been disconnected. The nuke would not explode.

Quinn looked up at the large digital-display screen on the command bunker's wall. The missile was still in the silo. It had not yet been launched.

In one of the screen's windows he caught sight of Griffin's running figure hastening through the tunnel linking the command-and-control center with the missile silo several hundred yards away.

Why was Griffin going there? Quinn's grenades had turned the launch capsule's operating system into a mass of heat-fused circuits and flash-melted silicon. There would be no launching the bird from there any longer. The infrastructure was completely gone.

Suddenly Quinn understood: Griffin had built a fail-safe mechanism into his plans to launch the missile. Griffin had a backup method of executing launch at his disposal, and this backup could be activated from the missile silo.

That's why Griffin was running down the tunnel. He was intending to execute a manual launch!

Quinn cradled the LSW bullpup and set off down the corridor after Griffin at a fast jog. The blast door separating the tunnel from the command center had been lowered, blocking access to the tunnel beyond.

Quinn's last two button charges blew the bulkhead to twisted metal debris.

Quinn rushed through the smoking wreckage of the blown steel panel into the dimly lit tube of reinforced concrete stretching below the Idaho landscape toward the Centerline missile silo at its opposite end.

Griffin was already inside the silo as Quinn entered the tunnel from the command-center side. Damaged though he was from the kinetic-energy fléchette strikes, the parahuman was still capable of carrying out the terminal phase of the operation.

Endgame was within reach.

Only minutes remained for him to success-fully launch the ICBM, and then the window of opportunity would close permanently.

If the nukes he'd planted in Moscow deto-nated before the launch signature of the Center-line was detected, then the sequence would not be recognized by ARGUS as a valid trigger param-eter and the global extinction that Griffin planned would not occur.

While Griffin began initializing manual launch procedures, Quinn was running toward the silo when a series of explosions suddenly shook the base.

After a second Quinn realized that the explo-sion in the command center must have affected the computer-controlled life-support machinery that cooled and heated the base and kept it sup-plied with air and water.

Fuel stores were now exploding from deep within the earth as shock waves penetrated through bedrock and natural fissures shifted un-der immense stress.

Huge, jagged fracture lines suddenly ap-peared on the tunnel walls and floor as Nomad felt debris rain down on his head. The floor shuddered violently for a moment, and he stum-bled and fell, picking himself up again to negotiate the last few hundred feet of corridor at a flat-out run.

Now Quinn could smell the acrid fumes of the liquid fuel seeping from the tanks of the rocket in the silo. The silo's bulkhead door was open, and he raced through onto the narrow catwalk circling the curving walls of the silo midway down the shaft.

He spotted Griffin on the other side of the towering missile, manipulating a keypad console set into the wall, then pulling down a stir-rup-type control lever, which produced immediate results.

Suddenly Quinn felt bright sunlight sting his eyes, which had become accustomed to the dimness of the access tunnel.

Looking up, he saw the huge circular silo blast door sliding back into its niche as hydraulic pistons pushed it aside.

Only seconds remained until the seventy-ton lid was fully retracted and the missile was launch capable.

Quinn made his way around the circular catwalk. Griffin sighted him then and targeted a burst of SMG fire his way.

Flattening against the silo wall for cover, Quinn fired back at Griffin, and the parahuman was temporarily knocked aside by the impact of the fléchettes.

Before Griffin could recover the initiative, Quinn darted to another part of the catwalk and launched pulsed multiround fléchette bursts at Griffin, catching him full on in a shock front of automatic fire.

The ballistic shock of the high-velocity rounds would have literally cut a normal human being to pieces, but the kinetic-energy bursts merely sent Griffin crashing into the wall of the silo, his hardened metal understructure absorbing most of the ferocious impact of the strikes.

Then Quinn ran out of ammunition.

The bullpup would no longer fire.

Recovering, Griffin brought up his own weapon and leveled it at Quinn as another severe tremor shook the underground installation to its roots. Griffin was pitched sideways so violently that he would have tumbled right over the edge of the catwalk railing and fallen to the bottom of the silo had he not dropped the SMG and grabbed the railing with his functional arm.

He dangled precariously beyond the edge of the catwalk railing, his fingers clawing at the steel struts as he held on with a single hand over a two-story plunge to the bottom of the pit.

Griffin looked up at Quinn and smiled. Hardly making any exertion, the cyborg began pulling himself up over the edge of the railing.

Nomad lunged for Griffin's dropped SMG lying on the floor of the catwalk a few feet away, picked it up and sprayed the contents of its clip into Griffin's face and torso before he could hoist himself up onto the metal ledge.

Griffin howled in rage and defiance, but his grip gave way under the impact of point-blank 10 mm fire, and he plummeted into the shadows below to land with a dull thud a heartbeat later.

On the silo command console Quinn saw the LCD readout indicate that only seconds remained until the ICBM was launched. There was no time to abort the launch via Griffin's override hardware now.

Quinn did not know Griffin's security code, and a few precious seconds lost attempting to access the microprocessor convinced Quinn that he would not find it in time to prevent the launch.

There was only a single option left to him at this point. Going for it, he pushed back the stirrup control, which would reclose the silo cover.

There was a pneumatic hiss and a steady mechanized drone as the blast door moved back into place over the mouth of the silo four stories overhead.

Shadows began to advance across the silo as daylight was blotted out and darkness fell in its place.

Quinn had now done all that he could. How the numbers tallied would determine the final outcome. Saving his own life, if he was able, was again a priority.

He climbed up the ladder that rose along one side of the circular pit and led all the way to the surface.

He had very little time left to climb to the top of the silo and pull himself over the edge before seventy tons of concrete and stressed steel closed around him and sealed him in, entombing him.

Struggling up the ladder, he hoisted himself up over the silo's rim and staggered to his feet scant seconds before the blast door closed behind him and was hydraulically locked in place.

He raced from the circular mouth of the silo with every ounce of power in his legs, knowing that the missile's boosters were already beginning to ignite and that the bird would now be lifting off.

In seconds the ICBM would collide against the closed silo shutter and blow itself apart. Quinn knew that safety features designed into the missile made it virtually impossible for a nuclear blast to occur under such circumstances.

But if he was too close to the epicenter of the explosion, there was no possible way he could survive. For Nomad the game's outcome would then be zero-sum.

FROM THE SLOPE-SIDED concrete floor of the silo, Griffin looked up at the sudden darkness, infrared vision in his one still-functional eye showing him the Centerline's huge tail cones.

The graphical user interface of his IVD made clear that only seconds remained before ignition of the massive booster rockets. He would never have sufficient time to abort the ignition.

Only to escape—if he could.

His left arm was smashed to useless pulp and his right eye had blanked out. But his legs were still functional, as was his intact right hand. He climbed the steel service ladder to the lip of the catwalk using his still-operational limbs, then raced through the open bulkhead and through the three-hundred-yard corridor beyond.

Suddenly there was the sound of a violent explosion as the missile's engine nacelles came to life with a demonic roar in the darkness of the silo.

Incandescent exhaust flame, which would normally be channeled through special blast nozzles directing it to the surface, now rushed directly into the tunnel itself.

Griffin put on a burst of speed, staying only seconds ahead of the deadly tide of superheated gases as he raced through the corridor.

Thunder now filled the tunnel as the missile crashed headlong into the closed silo shutter and blew itself apart in a violent paroxysm. Scorching fire and shattering blast waves traveled at high speed through the tunnel in a shock front of devastating power.

Griffin felt the intense heat at his rear, heat so great that it was making the back of his overalls begin to smolder as he outran the swiftly moving wave front. The heat seared the flesh on his back, singed off his hair and blistered the scalp of his surgically grafted cranial flesh.

Griffin reached the tunnel's opposite bulkhead as a tidal wave of fire sluiced into the base command center.

The parahuman was already crouching behind a heavy steel console as the battle cab turned into the white-hot nucleus of a zone of near-total burnout.

QUINN RAN; he ran and suddenly the world exploded **as** a balloon of fast-rising superheated gases rushed up from the flaming tube of the missile silo. The silo's massive concrete lid had suddenly burst into jagged pieces and flew up into the air to unbelievable heights.

The ground shook and shuddered violently beneath Quinn's feet, and he was propelled forward by a terrific blast of searing hot air that sent him hurtling through space.

The ground above the tunnel was caving in as he regained his footing and, with the odor of his own singed flesh in his nostrils, ran on and finally staggered toward the flashing lights indicating a cordon of emergency personnel that he had summoned to the base on arrival.

He did not know that beneath the heaving earth, Griffin was still alive and more dangerous than ever.

34

A black pall of toxic smoke hung over the Dutchman's Crossing installation, and flames were still spewing skyward in a fiery gusher, fed continuously by the thousands of cubic tons of fuel from both the ICBM's ruptured tanks and the underground reservoirs from which it had been pumped into the missile.

Carrying the small black cylinder he had retrieved from the flaming ruins beneath the surface of the rolling Idaho landscape, Griffin emerged from the ground-level room sixty feet above the burning command center, striding through the low-hanging clouds like a specter newly risen from the bowels of hell.

His still-functional IVD now in infrared-scan mode revealed that a state trooper wearing a gas mask was standing guard on the periphery of the blast zone.

The trooper could not see Griffin through the dense smoke clouds, nor could he hear him approach through the mask he wore and over the roar of the flames still geysering from the silo, but to Griffin's cybernetically augmented visual and audial senses, the trooper was clearly discernible.

Easily getting behind the trooper, Griffin slammed the heel of his palm into the base of the man's skull, smashing occipital bones and pulping nerve tunnels, causing instant death.

After his victim crumpled to the ground, Griffin changed into his uniform and covered his own badly mauled face with the gas mask.

Taking care not to get too close to the ring of emergency personnel that had besieged the installation and making maximum use of the trooper's mask to screen his ravaged face from view, Griffin made his way to the center of activity where command posts for the emergency units had been set up.

Only minutes before, an Osprey had landed from nearby Gifford Air Force Base. The VTOL—vertical takeoff and landing—plane fit perfectly into Griffin's immediate plans.

He made his way to the plane and pulled open its forward hatch. The pilot looked toward the masked figure in paramilitary fatigues who was preparing to board the aircraft.

"What can I do for you?" the pilot asked, a little puzzled, noticing that one arm seemed to dangle uselessly at the trooper's side.

Just as he noticed that the fingers of that arm were actually metal grapplers, Griffin was already inside the cockpit. A look of shock and horror registered on the pilot's face as he got an up-close look at Griffin's, but by then it was too late.

Griffin squeezed the pilot's throat and snapped his neck with his still-functional right hand. The pilot was then dragged into the rear of the plane and stuffed into a gear locker.

Griffin checked the VTOL's control panel and familiarized himself with the instrumentation. Flying the plane to his destination would pose no problem: his on-board programming already contained the necessary flight information and would walk him through whatever rough spots he might run up against in flight.

Griffin began warming up the jump aircraft's prop motors as he saw through the cockpit windscreen two men point at the plane and begin walking toward it. Griffin smiled as his IVD zoomed in on their faces for a close-up view.

He recognized one of the two men immediately: it was Quinn. He did not know that the second man was Casper Nordquist, head of Directorate Two-Zero and the very same agent who had been assigned to hunt him down, or that they had been discussing Lorimer's report from Moscow on the KGB's successful dismantling of the Russian nukes.

The second man pulled open the Osprey's hatch and climbed into the cabin of the plane. Quinn followed behind Nordquist, pulling the bulkhead door closed behind him and dogging it down.

"Let's go," Nordquist said to the man he believed was the plane's military pilot. Obviously the pilot had instructions to fly Quinn and the other man to some prearranged destination, Griffin realized then. He checked the aircraft's autopilot and found out precisely where that destination was: Washington, D.C.

It was tempting to know that all he had to do was sit back and let the aircraft fly him practically to the White House, but Griffin had another destination in mind.

He punched new coordinates into the onboard navigational computer as the plane rose vertically like a rotorcraft before its propellors shifted frontward for conventional flight at a distance from the ground of approximately sixty feet.

Now that the plane was airborne and well on its new course heading, Griffin could turn the controls over to the autopilot. When the plane was cruising at twenty thousand feet, he swiveled around in his chair to face his two passengers.

Quinn and the other man were talking as Griffin turned toward them. Quinn recognized Griffin first, tensing as he saw the ravaged features of the cybernetically augmented clone that had been his identical twin, though now, disfigured by fire and steel, was no longer even recognizable as anything remotely human.

The 10 mm Glock Griffin had confiscated from the trooper whom he'd wasted was already in Griffin's fist and pointing menacingly at his two passengers.

Nordquist, now staring at Griffin and muttering ''Oh, my God'' was reaching under his jacket for full-automatic hardware nestled there in a combat holster.

It turned out to be a rash move on his part.

The Glock barked savagely, and the Company man, wrenched around with his arms thrown outward, crumpled in a heap against the aircraft's bulkhead.

Having put down Nordquist, Griffin tracked the pistol on Quinn, who knew better than to test Griffin's computer-augmented aim, especially in such close quarters.

Quinn's glance flicked momentarily to the black cylinder now on the copilot's seat beside Griffin. It was the micronuke that Griffin had salvaged from the ruins of the missile complex, and Quinn knew that the special munition would not be with him now if he had not somehow rearmed and reprogrammed it.

"There is a change of plans," Griffin said. "Instead of Dulles, we're stopping much closer. The Rock River nuclear reactor complex will be our final destination."

"ARGUS has been neutralized," Quinn told the parahuman. "What's the point? Revenge? I didn't think your psychological conditioning made you capable of going for it."

"Revenge isn't my motive," Griffin returned, keeping the Glock trained on Quinn. "The source code from Iron Mountain included backup parameters for triggering ARGUS. Those parameters took into account the possibility of terrorist strikes using man-portable theater nukes. They are geared toward explosions of greater magnitude than this SADM produces, yes, but I think I can get around that limitation."

"You're mad," Quinn said, having grasped Griffin's purpose and not doubting that Griffin was correct and that he could pull it off. "It can't work."

"Yes," Griffin answered. "It can. It *will*. I've set this aircraft to automatically collide head-on with the main reactor dome of the Rock River complex.

"At that moment the micronuke will detonate. The combination of factors can and will cause a nuclear chain reaction, which I calculate will produce a nuclear detonation on the order of a ten-megaton blast. That's easily enough blast yield to trigger automatic retaliation by ARGUS."

Whether Griffin's last-ditch effort would succeed or not, it would still cause widespread destruction on a massive scale. Even a best-case scenario might include a *China Syndrome*-style meltdown that would make Chernobyl and the catastrophe at Mianwali, Pakistan, of 2001 look like dress rehearsals for Armageddon.

"Don't move," Griffin said as he saw Quinn tense with the realization of the new endgame's ramifications. "You wouldn't get far. We're both dead men now. What's important is that other Upcard parahumans will survive once ARGUS triggers doomsday. But you and I will die together. I find the symmetry of it appealing."

"Like placing the nukes in one Moscow and launching the missile from the other?"

"Yes," Griffin observed, suddenly realizing something. "That's what tipped you off, wasn't it?"

"It did," Quinn returned, determined to keep Griffin talking while he prepared to make a desperate move. Nordquist's machine pistol was lying nearby on the deck; he'd seen it out of the corner of his eye.

The plastic gun lay close at hand.

Cocked and locked, Nordquist had been telling Quinn just before boarding the VTOL—that's the way he liked to carry his blowback-driven piece.

But it might as well be a thousand miles away for all the good it would do. Griffin had him dead in his sights, and at point-blank range even a blind man would not be likely to miss with the Glock.

"You're barking up the wrong tree," Quinn said, stalling for time. "The nuke is a dummy, faithful in every detail except one—it contains no nuclear explosive. It's filled with a depleted-uranium core. You didn't really think I'd be foolish enough to risk my neck with a live SADM?"

"You're bluffing," Griffin answered, scanning Quinn's voice patterns for signs of stress but picking up mixed readings.

Quinn showed stress, yes. But whether or not such stress patterns indicated a lie from a man facing imminent death was beyond Griffin's ability to conclusively determine.

"Am I?" Quinn replied, carefully watching Griffin's face and steeling himself for the split second in which he would need to act or accept not only his own death but the deaths of countless millions. Quinn saw his moment arrive as Griffin flicked his eye toward the nuke beside him on the copilot's seat in an all-too-human reflex.

In that instant Quinn sprang into action, diving across the deck and grabbing at the butt of Nordquist's weapon as the hot pain of a Glock bullet entering his side flared through every nerve in his body.

Fighting back the intensifying pain, Quinn brought the machine pistol into sudden, violent play.

Positioned on the blind side of Griffin's damaged right eye, he succeeded in putting a burst into the clone's midsection, which knocked Griffin back in his chair and gave Quinn a chance to find cover behind cargo crates to the rear of the Osprey's passenger compartment.

Now Griffin held his fire.

He dared not risk throwing any more rounds into the pressurized cabin, dared not risk damage to the aircraft's instruments.

Shoving the Glock into his belt, he got up from the pilot's seat and moved balefully toward Quinn, who jumped from cover and emptied the machine pistol's magazine into Griffin's armored chest glacis.

Unharmed, Griffin tore the spent weapon from Quinn's fist with his single good hand. In retaliation, Quinn jacked hammering power punches at Griffin's stomach, which rocked him slightly but did not otherwise hurt him.

Brushing aside the punishing blows as if they were love taps, Griffin hurled Quinn against the Osprey's bulkhead with his functional hand, easily knocking the wind out of his weaker opponent. Bent on murder, he stalked toward Quinn, who lashed out with his final remaining reserves of strength and kicked open the latch of the aft bulkhead door.

All at once, there was a sudden, fierce suction as the pressurized air was ripped from the Osprey's cabin, sweeping Griffin irresistibly toward the plane's open hatchway, propelling the clone out into the Osprey's exhaust wash before his hand could gain purchase on the frame of the door.

Getting to his feet and struggling to reclose the hatch against the lessened but still severe pull of the wind, Quinn saw the already distant form of the tumbling body free-falling to the earth below, until Griffin shrank down in size to a tiny black speck and disappeared entirely.

Bleeding profusely, Quinn scrambled forward into the cockpit.

He had lied to Griffin.

The SADM was no dummy.

It was live and it was deadly, and Griffin had rearmed it. Quinn tried inputting his original access code sequence at the keypad below the readout panel but had no illusions that it would still work.

As expected, it didn't.

Griffin had deselected Quinn's original code, then replaced it with one known only to himself. The numbers on the nuke's LCD made it evident to Quinn that the SADM would explode in a matter of a few minutes.

Already Quinn could see the domes and funnels of the Rock River reactor complex gleaming in the sunlight below.

Quinn reset the VTOL's autopilot to take the plane higher into the air in order to gain as much altitude as quickly as possible.

Grabbing a parachute, he bailed out of the doomed aircraft, waiting until the last possible moment to pull the rip cord and open the chute so that every critical second spent in transit to the earth below would be minimized.

When the ground seemed about to swallow him up, Quinn pulled the rip cord and popped the chute.

Minutes later he hit the deck, unfastened himself from the chute harness and ran like hell for the shelter of a huge, lead-clad storm drainage pipe he'd spotted from the air.

The nuclear fireball ignited a moment or two after Quinn had taken cover, the shock wave of the low-yield airburst filling earth and sky with immeasurable sound and fury.

The SADM had been designed to produce a blast yield far smaller than that of the Hiroshima bomb, with a fraction of its radioactivity.

It had been designed to do its killing cleanly.

Quinn banked on that fact for his survival as the ground shook fiercely beneath him and knew that whatever the consequences of the nuclear airburst he had just set off, ARGUS itself would remain inactive.

The thousand-eyed technological monster created by misdirected men would not trigger the end of all life on the planet.

Whether he himself lived or died, at least Quinn had seen to that.

Justice Marshall Cade and his partner, Janek,
continue to bring home the law in Book 2 of the
exciting new future-law-enforcement
miniseries...

MIKE LINAKER

It takes a new breed of cop to deliver justice in tomorrow's
America—a ravaged world gone mad.

In Book 2: HARDCASE, a series of seemingly random murders
puts Cade and Janek on to a far-reaching conspiracy
orchestrated by a ruthless money manipulator and military
renegades with visions of taking over the U.S. government and
military.

Available in September at your favorite retail outlet.

**In the Deathlands, the only
thing that gets easier is dying.**

JAMES AXLER

DEATH LANDS ®

Moon Fate

Out of the ruins of nuclear-torn America emerges a band of warrior-
survivalists, led by a one-eyed man called Ryan Cawdor. In their quest
to find a better life, they embark on a perilous odyssey across the ravaged wasteland known as Deathlands.

An ambush by a roving group of mutant Stickies puts Ryan in the clutches
of a tyrant who plans a human sacrifice as a symbol of his power. With
the rise of the new moon, Ryan Cawdor must meet his fate or chance
an escape through a deadly maze of uncharted canyons.
